Complexities

A Novel By:

Kayla Isaac

WANT TO INTERACT WITH T'ANN MARIE & HER TEAM? JOIN OUR READERS GROUP ON FACEBOOK @ T'ANN MARIE PRESENTS: THE HOUSE OF URBAN LITERACY! WIN PRIZES, BE APART OF LIVE BOOK DISCUSSIONS & MORE!

Samya

"You're gonna make an ass of money tonight. Ballers always go for the young, new ones." Said Spice standing behind me in the mirror.

Looking back at my reflection, I tucked my lips in with multiple thoughts running through my head. If I didn't look seventeen before, the revealing two-piece I sported didn't support my argument at all. I was wearing a dark blue suede two piece that shimmered when light hit it, a pair of six inch clear pumps showcasing my freshly painted white toes, while my curly Afro was no longer visible due to the long jet black Brazilian bundles that flowed down my back. It was the first night I was put out on the floor, due to Spice training me a week prior.

She brought her head to my shoulder and smiled at our reflection in the mirror before pinching my cheeks.

"You ready?" She asked running her fingers through my hair. I felt as if she was more excited for me to get out there than I was nervous.

"Yeah."

"Good, now remember if you have any trouble call me." She replied pulling out my mask and placing it over my face. I nodded in response before following her out of the door.

The sound of Ro James' *Permission* blasted through the speakers as we made our way to the DJ stand. Walking through,

I received multiple looks from girls whose names I wasn't even aware of. My heart was doing cartwheels in my chest just from the thought of me getting on stage and attempting the moves I'd learned. The day I'd gone there I felt so sure of myself and now that it was time to get to work, I was on the verge of passing out. The fear that someone might figure out that I wasn't supposed to be there ran through me most of all. With Spice hooking me up with a fake ID and my stage alter ego, you would have thought my nerves would have been calm but they were far from it.

"Spice, Babydoll." Said the Dj, giving us a head nod.

"Jamie, as you know tonight is Babydolls first night. Play a little something that'll, you know."

"Ah, okay. Babydoll what you wanna dance to?"

"Surprise me." I replied causing him to raise an eyebrow at Spice, causing both of them to laugh.

"You comfortable already, I like that. Most of the new girls ain't as calm as you."

I nodded before Spice walked me behind the curtains. She turned me to face her before grabbing ahold of my shoulders.

"Remember what I said. It's like you're in your bedroom dancing in the mirror. You got this." She said pecking my forehead before walking off. Staring at the thick red curtains, my eyes wandered off to the pole as the bright lights shined through the peak.

"Tonight, we got a little something new for y'all. So, don't be afraid to show some love to our new girl Babydoll!" Jamie announced over the mic.

Summer Walker's *Girls Need Love* played through the speakers as the curtain began to open slowly. The fluorescent lights shined off of my skin as I looked up from the ground to the crowd of men. Something came over me, but all of the anxiety I had earlier seemed to have escaped my body as I gripped the pole, imagining that I was the only one in the room. The thought of me officially being my little sister's caregiver pushed me in that moment. Walking around the pole in circles I stopped with my back against the crowd, before slowly dropping down into a split, showcasing my ass.

As soon as the beat dropped, I began to twerk my ass while in a split before getting up and doing a few tricks on the pole, causing the crowd to go crazy. I didn't know if I was sweating more due to the bright lights and the heat, or my anxiety rushing back due to all of the eyes glued on me. By the time the song ended, the stage was already filled with ones, tens, twenties, and a few fifty-dollar bills. The bodyguard Eddie helped me gather my money from the stage before escorting me to the dressing room.

Emptying the plastic bag full of money on the vanity, I smiled in blithe. Even though I had to give forty percent to the manager, Vince, I was still happy that I was around so much money. I'd only been in Houston for two weeks and I'd been suffering. The majority of the money I had in front of me was sure enough going to take care of my half of the rent and food. Even though Spice insisted that I didn't have to pitch in, growing up I was always raised off of the saying, *you never get anything for free in this world.*

Due to me only being allowed to dance to one song on stage because it was my first night, I was already prepared to get the thong I was wearing out of my ass. As soon as I took my mask off Vince walked in with a Cheshire cat grin plastered on his face.

"Babydoll, Babydoll, Babydoll!" He smiled clapping his hands leaning on the doorframe.

"Wassup."

"For somebody with no experience in pole dancing, you sure as hell fooled me."

"I did two years of gymnastics and did creative dance for three years. It's pretty easy if you know what you're doing."

"Good. Well if your confident in yourself, I usually don't let new girls stay on the floor after one dance, but you can get back up. Plus, you got about ten requests for a private dance. I mean it's extra cash if your down?"

"I have to get home to my little sister soon, so I don't know."

"You sure?"

Twisting my lip to the side, a habit I had whenever I was deep in thought, I took a deep breath before thinking about how I needed to save up as much as I could to take care of my sister and I.

"I have time for one private dance, after that I have to go."

"Good! Just freshen up if you have to and make your way to room 9B."

I gave him a head nod watching him walk out the door. Looking back at my reflection in the mirror, I reapplied my lip gloss and put my mask back on, before hiding my money and walking out the doors. Greeting multiple strippers and men on my way to my destination, I stopped at the red curtain and took a deep breath before walking inside. The man that I stood in front of was sitting on the red plush couch, laid back with his hands behind his head. As soon as he noticed my presence, he lifted his head up, showing me his cognac colored eyes. As soon as the light hit his face completely, I felt intimidated by how good he looked.

His chiseled jawline, plump lips, and his muscular build made me hot as I stepped into the room. My eyes began to roam the tattoos that cascaded his arms like a canvas. I was so stuck in admiration that he was talking, and I didn't even hear any words escaping his lips.

"You stuck?" He asked tilting his head, snapping me out of

my daydream.

"Uh no, I'm sorry." I replied looking down feeling embarrassed.

"What you staring at the ground for?"

"I don't like making eye contact with people, it makes me nervous."

"So, I make you nervous?" He asked now standing up towering over my five-foot four frame. He at least stood at six foot four.

"No." I replied, backing up a little before he grabbed me by my waist.

"Aren't you supposed to be dancing for me?"

"Yeah."

I went to the touchpad on the wall before letting Drake's *Jungle* play, while I whined my hips to the beat of the music. Halfway into the song I noticed he wasn't even paying attention to me. He was just staring, off into space with an annoyed expression on his face. I didn't know if it was because of me or something else. Stopping the music, I raised an eyebrow before taking a seat by him.

"Is everything okay?" I asked genuinely concerned.

"Yeah."

"Look I know you don't know me, but don't lie to me. If you don't want to tell me that's all you had to say. I'm very good at reading people and I can tell when something is wrong with someone."

He sighed before running his hands down his face, playing with his beard. I caught a glimpse in his eyes and the hesitating expression plastered on his face.

"Aight I'd rather not talk about it." He replied simply before digging in his pocket and handing me three hundred, dollar bills.

"Well it's not good to hold in what's bothering you, your gonna explode sooner or later. Trust me I should know."

"And how would you know?" He replied sitting back on the couch with his arms crossed.

"Because I always wanted someone to be there for me to tell my issues to. One point I felt as if I would explode and trust me, it's gonna happen if you don't get what you gotta get off your chest."

He licked his lips before looking at me with hooded eyes. Placing his hand on my exposed thighs, he took a deep breath before clearing his throat. "I lost my kid two months ago." He said trying to hide the pain in his voice.

"I'm so sorry to hear that."

"Yeah, my son Micah. He was three years old; he would have been four today."

"Then what are you doing at a strip club? Shouldn't you be visiting your sons grave or finding other ways to cope."

"My girl put me out, she's taking it harder than me. I feel as if I'm at his grave every day and it don't make it any better for me."

"People cope differently. She just might need some time, just like you."

"Mcht, that's the thing. Every time there's a problem she run off. This isn't the time to run off, we need each other the most and this is what she do?" He replied failing to hide the crack in his voice. He looked down before I heard him sniffle. I grabbed his face and lifted it up to mine.

"Well somebody has to be strong in this situation and apparently, it has to be you. I know that it's hard being strong and people usually think that a man can't be torn down to un-recognition, but it happens. My dad always told me that somebody has to be there for the boulder when it cracks."

We stared at each other for what seemed like hours until he grabbed my chin and crashed his lips into mine. My natural reflex would have been to push the stranger off, but I just sat there stunned. It was my first time ever being kissed like that, especially by someone who was much older. His hands roamed from my waist to my butt, before he pulled away from the kiss. Running my hand up his shirt, feeling his hard abs, I felt my panties go damp. My finger traced the Bible verse tattoo on his side. As soon as he reached for my mask the curtains opened and Eddie stood there with a raised eyebrow.

"Times up!"

I stood up before attempting to walk off, but the guy grabbed my arm. Before Eddie could intervene, the guy gave me two more hundred-dollar bills before letting me go. After getting escorted back, I changed out of my clothes before looking down at the money in front of me, thinking about what I was going to do. What was my first move?

There I was, a 17, year-old stripper raising a 12 year-old. Just saying that in my head sounded maniacal. I knew it was time to grow up fast the day I'd stepped foot out of my mother's house. I'd had a feeling that I was going to succeed and start something new, but I knew it was hard. I always questioned myself on the decision I'd made. The choice of me dragging my little sister along with me when I rarely had my shit together. Was I better off back at home with an abusive stepfather and a drug addict mother? Was I strong enough to grow up fast and make big moves to do what it took to survive and provide for my sister and I?

My mind was rushed with thoughts like that every day that I woke up knowing I had to be someone my little sister could look up to.

Chapter 1: Homebound

Samya

<u>Six Years Later</u>

"Aunt Sasha, how many times do I have to tell you that I don't want to come back there. Jalisa and I are doing just fine here in Houston." I ranted trying to get ready for work.

"I know but come on. Your father is sick, and we need the both of you here for some type of support. You're still his daughter."

"That man is not my father. He's my mother's husband, let's keep it at that. He is Seven's father not ours."

"Well come down here for Seven; the least you can do is that, Samya."

"I'll think about it okay," I sighed running my hands through my hair.

"You always say you'll think about it. You've been gone for six years, Samya, you need to grow up."

"Bye, Aunt Sasha."

I clicked off the phone before looking outside at my neighborhood; staring off into space and thinking about how much I'd achieved. Thinking about how many years, hardworking years, it had taken me to get where I was.

"Yo, what you lookin lost for?" said my little sister, Jalisa, walking in with her keys.

"Nothing. Aunt Sasha called again."

"For what?"

"Trying to get us to come there because Will is sick."

"What that gotta do with us?"

"She wants us to come down there supposedly because he was asking about us."

"That man kicked us out and got mama hooked on God knows what. He thinks just because he put her through rehab and became a better person last year, that we're just gonna go back to him. Shit, we don't even talk to our biological father."

"He on some heavy shit if he thinks I'm going back there."

"Well I mean, a visit won't hurt. Not for him before you curse me out, but for Seven. We haven't seen him in years. I know you miss him."

"I've asked Seven to come here time after time and he won't, so whose fault is that?"

"Somebody has to be the bigger person, Mya."

"And that bigger person is me. Do you not remember what I went through being 18 trying to find a place for us? Trying to get us where we are now. I'm just now paying off my student debt. I've went through hell just to get us where we are right now! I had to build myself up mentally and emotionally to get us here. Just to make sure you don't have to go through what I went through at the age you are now."

"Okay, whatever Mya. I'm going to Chipotle with Zina and Ash. I'll see you whenever." She replied walking out, totally disregarding what I'd said.

I knew she was gonna be upset with me all day. At times

she'd agree with me about staying away from Baton Rouge and sometimes she grew curious and wanted to be around the family we'd left behind years ago. I watched her get into her Matte Black Jeep and drive off. Running my fingers through my hair, I made sure everything was situated in my home before grabbing my purse and heading to the salon I worked at. Getting in my Lexus ES, I drove off towards Keem's hair salon, that was on the other side of town. *Memories Back Then* blasted through my car until it was interrupted by my ringing phone. Rolling my eyes, I slid my finger across the screen hearing my cousin Una's voice ring through.

"I just got off the phone with your mama, I don't need another lecture."

"Hold up bitch, I'm not calling about that. I'm calling to warn you about something."

"Warn me about what?" I asked raising an eyebrow.

"Cam's mom been snooping around my job."

"What that gotta do with me?"

"She been asking about you."

"Saying what?" I replied wiping my sweaty palms, already nervous just hearing Cam's name.

"She was asking about her grandchild."

"What did you tell her?"

"I told her I haven't spoken to you since Camron went to jail."

"Thank you, I really don't feel like talkin to that woman."

"You need to call that woman and tell her the truth."

"I'll handle that another time."

"No, you need to tell her what went down."

"No! You know that lie is the only little bit of protection I have right now."

"Cameron has been in jail for the past six years, he has life in prison. No man should have that type of fear over you, Mya. You literally living life paranoid!"

"I'm the reason he's in jail, Una."

"You technically didn't lie."

"But I snitched on him."

"Either you stay and let him beat the shit outta you, or you do what you did. He deserves to be in jail."

"I don't know, Una. It's just sometimes I worry about what if he ever gets out and his first trip is to get me. Especially if he finds out what I did?

"He's not, and if he does, he gotta get through me."

"I love you, Un." I smiled before quickly wiping my eyes.

"I love you too, My-My. But I also need to talk to you about Nana."

"What about her?"

"I took her to her last doctor's appointment today and her breast cancer is getting worse."

"Are you kidding me? I paid for the best of the best for her and nothing is working?"

"Mya, money don't solve all the issues."

"I know, it's just I try so hard to help her."

"I know you don't want to be here but before she's not here anymore, I think it'll be a good surprise for her to see you."

"Come on Una, I thought you said you weren't calling to-."

"I wasn't calling to get you back here but that was something that needed to be relayed to you. Nana doesn't like when I alert people about her condition, but you need to know since you're the one paying for her hospital bills and chemo."

"Una, I'll think about it okay."

"You don't have all the time in the world to think. Mya you need to get over this fear that you have. Just come down for a week and then you can go back home to your lavish life that you have in Houston."

"As I said, I'll think about it, Una. I'll call you later; kiss Nana for me."

Before she could say anything else, I hung up and pulled my car into my usual parking spot. After checking my makeup in the rearview mirror, I got out and the men on the sideline did their usual hoots and hollers whenever I came into work. Ever since I'd began working in the area I'd become known as the curvy young black woman, that lived in the hills with the white people. Even after six years of being there, it was still my title.

"Roxanne, Roxanne I wanna be yo man." Sung Benny the liquor store owner.

"Hey Benny." I laughed giving him a wave.

"Hello, Miss Mya. How you doin today?"

"I'm doing pretty good and you?"

"I'm doin fine. My son asked about you yesterday."

"Of course, he did." I laughed.

"I'm serious. He is supposed to be stopping by and getting a lineup today. You should give him a chance."

"I don't know, Benny, I'm not looking for a man right now."

"Then he'll be a good friend."

"Bye, Benny." I laughed walking into the salon/barbershop.

"Is that my favorite girl, Samya?" Said my boss Kareem.

"Hey." I smiled bringing him into a hug.

"Hey boo, listen I'ma need you to work a double today. I have to make a three-hour drive outta town to get us some new product and meet up with some investors."

"Okay, I can do that."

"I can always count on you, hun. Thank you."

"You're welcome be safe on that road."

"I will." he replied bringing me into another hug and kissing my cheek, before digging into his pocket for his keys. He waved goodbye to everyone before walking out of the building.

I went over to the IPad and went to notes to see who was scheduled next.

"Is Mariah here?" I called out.

"Here." she replied getting up from her seat and coming to the styling chair.

Taking her bonnet off I looked at the IPad to see she wanted box braids. While doing her hair I listened in on the salon gossip. Everyone's eyes went to the door as soon as the bell alerted them that someone was coming in.

"Hey, Jay." Said all, of the ladies in unison with nothing but lust in their eyes. I looked over at the door where Benny's son Jay stood in athletic attire.

"Hey ladies." He smiled showing his grill.

There was no doubt that Jay was a fine man. He owned his own tattoo shop and soul food restaurant spot. He was genuine and was persistent when it came to something he wanted, and I'd learned that by the multiple attempts to get at me. He approached me and licked his lips before extending his hand.

"Nice seeing you again, Mya." He smiled.

"Same here. My boy Keven can line you up. Your dad said that's what you were coming in for."

"I also came in to talk to you."

"Okay we're talking now." I laughed lightly.

"I know, but can I have a word with you alone?"

"Anything you wanna say to me, you can say it in front of everybody; we're like family." Everybody gave us the eye with anxious faces.

"Aight, I'm tryna take you out tonight. Are you down? Or do I have to get on my knees and beg you?"

I looked around and everybody was as anxious for an answer as he was. I tucked my lips before looking into his eyes, seeking his intentions.

"I have to work a double shift, I'm sorry."

"No, she doesn't. I'll take over." Said my coworker, Bri, coming over to finish Mariah's hair.

I gave her a look that could kill and all she did was smile and push me away. Jay held out his hand awaiting on me to take it. Hesitant I shook my head no and pushed Bri out of my spot

"I promised him I would do this double. How about you treat me out to breakfast tomorrow?" I smiled.

"I'll take it." He smiled, before going off to Kevin to get his lineup.

As soon as I touched Mariah's hair my phone went off. Preparing myself to ignore my aunt and Una's call, I answered when I noticed it was Jalisa.

"Wassup, I'm at work right now make it quick."

"You need to come home, right now!"

"I can't, Jalisa, I have to work a double."

"Seven's here."

My breath automatically got caught in my throat and I'd suddenly forgotten how to breath. As bad as I wanted to see my brother, I never knew how I was going to react. I hadn't seen Seven in six years and for him to pop up unannounced after many failed attempts for me to get him here, was beyond me. For some odd reason I was scared, I was nervous, and I didn't know why. Was it because a part of me knew I had to face my brother one way or another? I had to finally face the brother that I'd left behind with a crack fiend mother and an abusive, manipulative father.

"Hello, Mya, you there?" Asked Jalisa catching my attention.

"Uh yeah, I'm on my way."

"Please hurry up."

"Ok I'm coming." I hung up before grabbing my bag and looking over at Bri. "You remember when you said you would work my double? Well here you go."

"Wait, what? Why?"

"I have a family emergency at home."

"Oh okay, no problem. Just text me if everything's okay."

"I will, thanks."

Waving goodbye to everyone, I went to my car and drove straight home, with a million questions running through my head like a marathon. It may have sounded ludicrous, but I was indeed scared to come face to face with my brother. The first thing that came to mind, was that he was going to blame me for everything. Blame me for leaving him to fend for himself at such a young age. Something I didn't want to do but had no choice but to do.

Pulling into my yard, I killed the engine and swallowed the huge lump in my throat, wiping my sweaty palms. Grabbing my purse, I got out. With every step I'd taken closer to my house, the more nervous I'd became. Before I could twist the knob and open the door myself, it swung open revealing my brother with a sly smug on his face.

"Well, well, well, long time no see." He said leaning on my door frame with his arms crossed.

Chapter 2: The Guilt

Samya

I sat across the table from Seven as if it was some kind of business meeting. It seemed as if I couldn't find the words to say to him. All I could do was stare at him and admire how much he'd grown into his looks and how tall he'd gotten. The fourteen year-old boy that I'd left back in Baton Rouge was now twenty years old, with facial hair and muscles. Looking into his face, all I saw were memories of my mother in his eyes.

"I didn't come over here for you to stare me down like I'm some kind of stranger." he said tilting his head to the side and leaning back with his arms crossed. The first thing I knew for sure, was his demeanor was far from how it used to be. He looked cold and hard from the inside out.

"Sorry, just haven't seen you in years."

"Well, surprise."

"What are you doing here?"

"Never knew I needed an invitation to see my sisters."

"You don't."

"Okay, then apparently I'm here for a reason."

I looked over at Jalisa who was leaning on the counter

looking down. I could tell Seven's visit had caught her off guard as much as it did me. Whenever she felt nervous, she always avoided eye contact the best she could.

"Then what's the reason?" I asked trying to keep my composure for the sake of Jalisa, since I knew she had questions that she was too afraid to ask.

"To talk because apparently you still giving the family the cold shoulder."

"You fucking serious right now?" I scoffed getting out of my chair and looking at him sideways.

"Yes, I'm fucking serious right now. I'm not Una or Aunt Sasha so I'm not about to kiss your ass about the entire situation. You're a grown woman right? Then sit down and talk like one, instead of running; since it seems to be your go-to."

I clenched my fist before walking up on him, causing him to get up from his chair. Jalisa ran in between us before anything could lead to anything further.

"Okay, look, I think you guys need to calm down before-."

"Before what? Her ass finally decides to grow the fuck up?!"

"Shut the fuck up! You don't even know what the fuck you're talking about!"

"Then enlighten me, Mya!"

"I'm sorry okay!" I yelled trying my hardest to keep my voice from cracking. He looked into my eyes before shaking his head and chuckling.

"Save them tears for the birds, man." he said throwing his hands up and walking away.

Jalisa followed behind him with tears running down her face as well. I could tell she was feeling some type of guilt when I was the one who had all the guilt on my back. I heard the front door slam and Seven arguing with Jalisa in the front yard. I walked over to the side before wiping my eyes and calming my nerves. As soon as I looked out the window again, I could hear Jalisa pleading for Seven to stay.

"Don't let him work you up."

I turned around to be face to face with my older brother Jamir. As soon as I saw him, I ran into his arms and he embraced me into a hug. I didn't know if I was crying harder for the fact of the situation I was in, or that I was finally in the presence of my older brother whom I hadn't seen in years either.

"Stop crying, it's not that serious, aight?" he said rubbing my back.

"No man, it's just I can't do-."

"Yes, you can do this, and this talk was long overdue. It's time for you to get over this shit, Samya."

I took a deep breath keeping my head on his chest, with my arms around his waist. He pulled away before staring down into my eyes, looking for my next move. He knew Seven was the hot head of the family and I was the impatient one. That was another reason I knew a sit down between Seven and I wasn't going to go anywhere.

Jalisa came back in with Seven in front of her and a look of aggravation written on her face. I knew it had taken a lot to get him back in the house and by the look on her face, you could tell it was a struggle. Jamir sat us down at the table again; he scoffed and looked away from me before I shook my head and wiped my tears away.

"So, who's going first?" asked Jalisa with her arms crossed.

Seven and I gave each other a death glare before looking away from each other again.

"Look, I'm just gonna start, aight?" Said Jamir taking a deep breath and stroking his beard. "Look Mya, everything at home is going left. Even though I don't live in Baton Rouge anymore, I do visit the best I can and shit looking pretty rough right now. Will just found out that he has lung carcinoma. He wants all of us to come to Baton Rouge to support him through his chemo."

"No."

"Bitch," mumbled Seven.

"Look, I've had enough of your shit!" I yelled getting up causing him to stand up again. It was pretty evident that if Jamir and Jalisa weren't there, Seven and I would have been fighting like dogs.

"Then what the fuck you gonna do about it?!"

"Chill the fuck out!" yelled Jamir loud enough that his voice damn near had the house rumbling.

Growing up I knew to never cross my older brother when he was serious and Seven knew the same. Seven and I looked at Jamir at the same time before sitting back down and giving Jamir our full attention.

"I'm not about to fucking sit here and play mama and daddy for you two. I got three got damn kids of my own and they don't argue as much as you two. Samya you're twenty-four years old, you need to grow the fuck up and stop this got damn act you got going on. Seven, look man, I know you been through some shit but you twenty years old right now and you acting like a bitch. Give the girl some time to talk. You can't force nobody to do shit and that same fucking temper of yours, is gonna get you in some trouble. If I gotta stop the both of y'all one more got damn time, lord so help me somebody better go ahead and have the fucking police down the road to haul my ass out of here."

You could see the vein in Jamir's forehead twitching, as his jaw clenched, letting us know he was far from playing any games. Seven took a deep breath before wiping his hands down his face, looking at me with nothing but hurt in his eyes.

"I was fourteen when you left me, man." his voice cracked.

"I had to sit there and keep mama off that shit; I had to make sure my damn dad ain't kill her ass half the time! It was me who held our family together when you up and left. Not only did I hold our fucking family together to the best of my ability, but I waited on you! You told me you were going to come back for me, but you never did. You know he broke my rib and my arm, right? He did that to me when he found out that I was going to leave him, just like all three of you did! He got his shit together when he almost killed me and broke my ribs again; the second time it punctured my lungs. It took for him to almost kill his child and his ass to get cancer to get his shit together!"

"Seven I-."

"I don't want to hear shit you have to say! I'm just here to get this shit off my chest and head back home. For you to be my big sister, you got a funny way of showing it. Look at where you live, man. Look at what you got! I live in a trailer, working two jobs, trying to pay for rent and tuition. I help mama pay rent and to top everything the fuck off, my depression is kicking my ass! You know what? The entire time my dad had been drilling it in my head that you left with Jalisa because y'all got the same damn dad and I'm starting to believe that shit! He told me every day that you ain't give a shit about me! You took her and you left me like I was nothing! And don't even lie to me and say you got kicked out because you didn't, and I know you didn't. I just wanted to look you in your face and tell you how much of a liar and a fucking bitch you are! You left me with a drug addict mother and an abusive father and took Jalisa like she was the only one who needed to be saved. Then, you not only have the nerve to leave, but you living like this and never came back to get me. I don't even know what to think about you anymore."

He stood up and walked out before I could even say anything. As soon as I tried to stand up, Jamir motioned for me to sit back down. I looked over at Jalisa who held nothing but tears in her eyes. She looked over at me and shook her head before walking off. I could hear her room door slam which made my heart drop.

"Look, give him some time to calm down. I'm here for you and I want you to know that." said Jamir placing his hand on top of mine.

"Jamir, he doesn't know what I've be-."

"I know he doesn't know. But you need to give him some space, alright? Seven's been through some shit and I know it's hard hearing the truth, but you need to know."

"No! He needs to know the fucking truth! He's not the only one who had to face some shit!" I yelled with my bottom lip trembling.

"Look, I know what happened, that's all that matters right now. I'll tell Seven whenever it's the right time."

"I didn't mean to leave him alone, Jamir, and you know that. I couldn't get him even if I tried."

"I know." he replied looking down holding onto my hand.

"Look, Aunt Sasha is holding this lil get together for Nana's seventieth birthday next week. I'm not forcing you to come home because you a grown woman and by the looks of it, you already got shit going for yourself here. I just think it'll be a good surprise for Nana to see you."

"I'll think about it, J."

"Good." He replied standing up and coming over to kiss my forehead.

"We'll be staying in The Post Oak Hotel; we leave in two days."

I nodded before giving Jamir another hug and walking him out. Once we reached the middle of the yard, I looked into the car to see Seven looking off into space. After watching Jamir and Seven leave, I went back inside and made my way to Jalisa's room. Approaching her door, before I could knock, her door swung open revealing her with bags in her hand.

"Where are you going?" I asked following behind her.

"To stay with Ash for a few. I need to clear my head."

"Are you serious right now?"

"Yes, I'm serious."

"Can I explain som-."

"There's nothing to explain. I don't know what to believe about you right now. You're so shut in that you don't let anyone in and it's becoming real, selfish. I'll be back home whenever I'm in the mood."

She brushed passed me and I didn't even bother running after her. As soon as I heard the front door close and her drive off, I walked into the living room and sat down on my couch, calling my cousin Cherish.

"Hm, Seven must have already made it there?"

"So, you knew and didn't think to call and tell me." I said in disbelief.

"Look, you barely answer whenever I call, so don't act surprised. What happened?"

"A lot happened. Seven is pissed off with me and Jalisa left to stay at a friend's house."

"I mean, we all knew he was going to be pissed off with you, that was evident."

"It's just, I tried so hard to keep this bullshit away from here and here it comes charging at me with full force."

"That's the thing, you always seem to distant yourself from shit that you know that you need to face, and you need to work on that because it's not a good look. You've been doing that shit for the longest and it's time to let it go."

"Fine, what do you want me to do?"

"I would have thought that you would have seen a therapist by now about this. And I don't have time for you to lie and say don't need one because you do. Half the shit you been through I would need help too. Sometimes superwoman needs a break too, you know?"

"Thanks, Cherish."

"Don't thank me for telling you something you should already know."

"Can you do me a favor?"

"Depending on what it is because I'm broke and got bills to pay."

"Can you clear out my old room at Nana's place?"

"So, you finally coming?"

"Seems like I have no choice."

"You always have a choice."

"That's what they always say. Just keep this on the low for me, please?"

"I got you."

"Thank you."

I hung up before taking a deep breath and looking up at the ceiling with my eyes closed. It took everything in me to make that decision and I knew for sure that the guilt that was taking over my soul, was going to be worse when I arrived.

Chapter 3: Where it All Began

Samya

It was officially the last day that Seven and Jamir would be staying in Houston, before going back to Baton Rouge. The entire visit Seven and I hadn't spoken a word to each other nor had Jalisa returned home. I was currently sitting in my living room with Jamir since he was the only one who was willing to talk to me and didn't see me as the bad guy.

"How you feel?" he asked watching me zone out. Something I'd found myself doing since the whole ordeal.

"I'm fine, just thinking."

"Talk to me."

"Just thinking about CJ." I smiled weakly clearing my throat to keep it from cracking.

"What about him?"

"Una said Cam's mom has been snooping around asking about him."

"So, what you gonna do?"

"That's the thing, I don't know what to do."

"I've told you time after time, you need to go see somebody. After going through what you went through, shit, I would need some help too."

"It's just, I feel like it's my fault that he's no longer here." I replied quickly swiping away my tears. I knew they were coming because whenever I'd talk about CJ, it was all I could find myself doing.

"It's not your fault."

"Yes, it is. And the fact that only you and Una know what I did, it's just sometimes I think about what 1-."

"Stop self-pitying yourself, alright. Look promise me something. Whenever you get time, go see a therapist or something. I know I'm your brother and you're looking for help in me, but you need professional help. I can't provide you with the same response someone else can. All you do is come to me and tell me the same thing, over and over again. You never tell me about good shit and that's one of your biggest issues. You always look for the bad to the point where you can never talk about the good. I tell you this shit all the time."

I looked over at him with nothing on my mind to say. I knew he was right, and I couldn't come up with a snarky remark or an attitude to go against him. He grabbed his jacket and threw on his slides before pulling me out of my seat and into a hug.

"Look, I gotta go and hit this road. Take what I said into consideration, please."

"I will." I smiled weakly before tucking my lips in.

"Good, keep in touch."

I nodded watching him walk out of the door. Once his car sped off, I went into my bedroom and began packing my bags. Running my hands through my hair I could feel the uneasiness in my stomach and my heart felt as If it was beating one thousand miles per minute. Picking up my phone I decided to text Jalisa instead of calling, already knowing she was going to send me to voicemail. After thinking things through, I decided I wanted to go to Baton Rouge alone, being unaware on how things would go if I'd brought Jalisa along. Knowing the situation we were already in, I knew she was going to be even more furious than she was now. After shooting her a text, I finished with packing my luggage, then shot Kareem a text stating I wasn't going to be at work for a week.

I found myself going to my secret stash and pulling out a bag of weed, Maui Pineapple Swishers, and a lighter.

"Hey Alexa, play New Balance by Jhene Aiko." I said, in the midst, of breaking down my weed. Jhene Aiko's angelic voice sounded through my speaker systems as I rolled up my well needed blunt. Grabbing my Bic lighter from the glass ottoman, I sparked up my blunt not even bothering to grab air freshener to hide the scent from Jalisa. I couldn't remember the last time weed touched my lips. Closing my eyes, I inhaled the smoke before exhaling and licking my lips. All the pressure and the frenetic rush from my anxiety was lifted off of my shoulders in a matter of minutes.

"Most of us are hurting. Most of us are searching, someone to love, someone to understand." I sang with my head tilted back and my eyes closed.

I was so in the zone that I didn't even hear my best friend, Renny, come in.

"Bitch I know you heard me banging on the door like I'm the fucking police." He said thumping me in my forehead and tossing his Louis Vuitton purse on the couch across from me.

"I didn't hear you."

"Well good thing I wasn't the fucking police because yo ass would have been in jail."

I simply responded with a shoulder shrug before taking one more pull from my blunt. Since I knew Renny was going to interrupt my personal session, I decided to cut it short and put out my blunt, saving it for later.

"Uh uh, what's wrong heffa? You in here listening to Jhene

Aiko depressing ass, smoking like a stressed-out single mother of six kids."

"I don't feel like talkin about it right now." I replied hoping he would drop it, but I knew he wasn't.

"I don't give a fuck what you don't feel like doing. Now answer my question. Why you up in here lookin like yo husband done left you for me."

"So, my brothers dropped by."

"Oh, the sexy one. Shoot what's his name again?" He asked himself, getting excited just from the mention of my brother.

"Jamir."

"Yes, his fine ass. I would nut all in that man."

"See, this is why I don't tell you shit."

"My bad, I'm listening. What about him?"

"He and Seven dropped by."

"Oh God. How did it go, My?" He asked getting serious and pulling my hands in his.

"It could have went better. All this time I've been wanting to know how my little brother felt and he basically hates me, you know? I mean who wouldn't hate me, look at the type of person I am." I replied quickly wiping away fresh tears that were forming on the brim of my eyes.

"Stop that shit! You've come a long way from where you used to be, I'll be damned if I sit here and watch my best friend break like this. What happened to all that confidence from last week?"

"It all went down the drain."

"Well you better dive in and race after that bitch. I don't care what happens or who try and make you feel any different. You're a bad bitch and don't let anybody tell you otherwise. Fuck what your siblings think. If they're interfering with your happiness and joy then you need to x they asses out! And that goes for Jalisa too. Shit even me. I know you've been wanting that closure from your brother but don't let it ruin you like it did then."

"That's why I love you." I sniffled and laughed lightly, pulling him into a hug.

"I love you more, Mya."

"I wish you could come with me to Baton Rouge to keep my head on my shoulders for me."

"Hold up, I know I'm not drunk. Go where?"

"I decided to go visit for a week or so. Just like you told me a few months ago, I need to work on getting closure for myself. I've been hiding way too long, so I decided to go."

"I'm happy for you. Look at you getting your shit together."

"Always."

"So how does Jalisa feel about it?"

"I'm not telling her I'm going."

"Then what's your excuse? Can't wait to hear this bullshit lie."

"Going out of town to visit a friend."

"Bitch what friend? You know you can't use me because I'm a hoe and I stay in the streets, so, she's gonna see me regardless."

"I'll make one up." I replied rolling my eyes.

"Mhmm, you got this all figured out, huh?"

"Somewhat."

"Lord, what am I gonna do with you? So, when you leaving?"

"Probably early tomorrow morning. It's a three damn near

four, hour drive."

"You need help packing?"

"Yeah."

"Good, so since your leaving me for a week, I brought cele- bratory Henny." He smiled pulling a bottle of Hennessy Cognac Xo from his purse.

"When is there a day that you don't drink?" I laughed shak- ing my head.

"On Sunday. That's the lord's day, I be in church. But some Sundays I have my lil share of wine."

"You going to hell." I laughed.

"Well, apparently I'm going to hell regardless if I'm an al- coholic or not." He laughed lightly before looking down.

"What's wrong, Ren?" I asked quickly noticing the change in his reaction.

"Girl, nothing." He replied getting up and going into the kitchen with the bottle. Following behind him I watched him pull two shot glasses from my Mahogany cabinets and place them on the white marble countertop.

"You helped me when I needed advice so I'm gonna return the favor. What's up?"

"My mother called last night and told me that my father has Arrhythmia. I wanted to stop by and check up on him but apparently he still doesn't want to see his *queer* son."

"He'll come around."

He scoffed before taking his shot to the head and pouring another. "That man has a serious heart disease and could die. He could die any day and still wouldn't want to be around me."

"Well, look at the bright side. You have a Master's degree in Business and have your own company. You're an amazing artist and photographer, not to mention you have a great personality."

"It's just, growing up I tried to meet my father's expectations but now that I know that he can pass away at any moment, it's really hitting me."

"I know. Just know it's gonna be okay."

"Duh, we got this girl. We got this." He smiled pulling me into a hug.

Renny and I spent the entire afternoon drinking and binge watching the Purge movies and series on Netflix. Once it was time for Renny to head home, I was left by my lonesome once again. I sat in my bed watching the fluorescent light from the moon reflect off of my cream wallpaper. Staring down at my packed Gucci suitcases, I took a deep breath and glanced at my clock, seeing that it was 2:45 in the morning.

"You got this." I mumbled to myself before pulling the covers over my body and going to sleep.

Chapter 4: Reminisce

Samya

"How long are you gonna be gone?" Asked Jalisa leaning on her door

"About a week."

"Why so long?"

"Because I haven't seen my friend in years."

"Mhm, why couldn't she come here?"

"Why so many questions?" I laughed hencing the tad bit of worry in her voice.

"Because after all that happened with Seven, you're going out like it never happened?"

"Well what do you expect me to do, Jalisa? Sit at home all day thinking about how my little brother dogged me out?"

"Have a safe trip." She scoffed, closing the door in my face.

Sighing, I grabbed my keys and made my way to Jalisa's door. Twisting the knob to see that it was locked, I shook my head in annoyance.

"I'm heading out. I'm gonna call you and have Ren check up on you until I get back. Please be safe and try to stay in contact with me, Lisa."

"Bye Mya."

"I love you."

Expecting a response back, she simply turned her tv up, completely ignoring me. Deciding to leave it be, I got into my silver Lexus ES, preparing myself for the life changing journey ahead of me. Looking at the time on my radio that read 5:30 AM, I pushed my push to start button and pulled out of my paved driveway. Looking out my rearview mirror as I drove away from my house, all I could think about was how much faster I could come back. I couldn't remember the last time I'd left Jalisa home for any period of time. Since Jalisa was fresh out of high school and started her freshman year of college at Spelman University in two months, I was hesitant about leaving her alone.

The entire ride to Baton Rouge made my stomach turn like a spin wheel. I couldn't believe I was actually back in the place that caused me so many nightmares. Passing the *Welcome to Baton Rouge* sign, the nostalgia started to kick in like a drug. I smiled seeing the same park that Jamir, Seven, and I shared so many memories. The memory of Jamir getting me to beat up a little girl who he knew he couldn't hit, ran across my mind. I remembered it all as if it was yesterday. The sun beaming down on my shiny forehead, due to my mother always applying to much hair grease whenever she did my hair. Me running around across the red and brown wood chips, that caused me to skin my knee on multiple occasions. Jamir pulling me off of the monkey bars, practically dragging me under the almond tree that had more almonds on the ground than on the tree. Last but not least, the memory of Jamir attempting to make me fight some little girl for him, when I've never fought a day in my life. It amused me remembering how he told this one girl that I would dog walk her ass up and down the park.

I soon passed by my grandmother's bakery and even with my windows cracked partially, I could smell my grandmother's recipe of cinnamon strawberry cheesecake cookies. Those cookies were like crack, and half of Baton Rouge were junkies for them. All, of my beatific memories slowly began to fade away when I drove into my old neighborhood. Our family was so close that we all lived in the same neighborhood and was walking distance from each other. I bypassed the various men rolling dice on the sidewalk and kids running around through sprinklers to beat the summer heat.

Finally pulling into my Nana's driveway, I killed the engine and took a deep breath, looking up at the two-story brick house. Opening my door, I got out of the car. The closer I stepped to the door, the closer my heart was pushing out of my chest. Knocking on the screen door, I was just praying that no one was home.

"If it's Jehovah's Witness I already told y'all people we good and ain't interested!"

I knew that voice from anywhere. I smiled just from hearing my cousin Una's loud, thick, Southern accent. As soon as she came to the door, her exasperated expression soon turned into glee. She swung the door open and ran out hugging me, damn near tackling me off of the porch onto the concrete.

"Please tell me I'm mother fucking dreaming because ain't no got damn way!" She yelled squeezing the life out of me.

All I could do was laugh as my cheeks began to ache just from smiling so hard. As soon as she pulled away from the embrace, I didn't even recognize that I was crying full blown tears.

"I missed you so much, Una." I said bringing her back into the hug, rocking her with me. I embraced the smell of her Chanel Coco scented perfume. She pulled away again before wiping the stray tears from my cheeks with her thumb. I was such a fucking water bag and I hated it.

"I missed you too. What are you doing here? I thought you said you weren't coming after what we talked about on the phone."

"I never said I wasn't coming."

"Could have fucking fooled me the way you were acting."

"I had a change of heart."

"Mhm, well Nana's gonna be so happy when she sees you."

"Is she home?"

"Nah, she's at the salon getting her hair done, she's going to a wedding tomorrow."

"Oh okay. Well is my old room still available?

"Girl no, that's the storage room now. I can clear it out for you if you wanna stay here or you can stay with me."

"I'd rather be here to help Nana out. I can clear the room out myself. I could have sworn I told Cherish to do it."

"You sure?"

"I'm positive." I smiled.

Una and I grabbed my suitcases and made our way inside. As soon as I stepped foot inside, the scent of cinnamon and vanilla filled my nostrils. A smile crept on my face when I noticed the only thing that changed in the house, was the minor change in furniture. The crimson colored walls were aligned with family photos, diplomas, and Degrees. I stopped in my tracks noticing the photo of my mother holding me just after giving birth. Even after going through labor my mother looked like an angel with a glow as bright as the sun. It pained me to see that my mother didn't look truly how she did then. Her long brown curly hair was now in the style of a blonde buzzcut and her hazel eyes were always covered with green contacts.

"You good?" asked Una, watching me admire the photos on the wall.

"Yeah, just thinking."

"Well, get your head out of the clouds and let's go clean this room for you." she replied throwing her arm over my shoulder and heading towards the room.

As soon as I opened the door, nostalgia hit me once again. My queen-sized bed was covered with boxes and old clothes. I laughed to myself looking at my walls, noticing the Beyonce' and Lauren Hill posters plastered in every corner. It took Una and I close to an hour to clear out my room and have walking space. Now that everything was cleared out, I could finally unpack my things and relax.

"Yo, you wanna go to Nino's to get something to eat? I don't know if you got something to eat on your way here or not?"

"Eh it don't matter." I replied hesitantly.

I wasn't even going to lie and say I wasn't tired since I'd left early, and I was on the road for a couple of hours. Not to mention the last thing I wanted to do was be seen by anyone.

"You sound a little uneasy with that answer, you sure?"

"Yeah, plus I'm hungry and I don't know what time Nana's is gonna be back to cook, if she cooks."

"Alright, you wanna take my car or yours?"

"Doesn't matter to me."

She rummaged through her pockets before pulling out the keys to her blue Jeep Wrangler. Grabbing my wallet and cell phone, I followed Una to her car. Getting inside, she pulled out of the driveway heading towards Ninos.

"So, tell me cousin, how does it feel to finally be here, you know?" She asked glancing at me with a smile then back to the road.

"I don't feel as nervous as I thought I would be."

"Good. Because you was stressing for nothin and I've been telling you that for the longest."

"I know, it's just I still kind of have this feeling that I've been trying to shake away ever since I got off the exit to get here."

"Well you can shake that feeling by shaking some ass to-night with me and Dezzy." She laughed nudging me, trying to make me smile.

"I ain't been here for a whole day and you tryna have me in a club already?"

"When was the last time your ass even been out to a club?"

"I haven't been to a club since I've stopped stripping."

"Damn, well you're going out with us tonight then."

"I think not! I'm gonna chill at home with Nana and then later on this week, you can take me out."

"Fine." she pouted.

"Fix your face before I fix it for you." I laughed, plucking her in the forehead.

She scrunched her face up before pulling into Nino's park-ing lot. We got out before going inside. Before we could even sit down fully, I heard my name surface from someone's mouth.

"I must have woken up from a coma, is that little Mya?" said the manager walking from behind the counter and coming towards me with open arms. I smiled walking into his arms and letting him embrace me.

"Hey Eddy." I grinned letting him go.

"How you been? It's been years, I haven't seen you since you were this high." he laughed holding his hand up.

"I've been good."

"Your mama just left here not long ago. Does she know you're here?"

"No, she doesn't know I'm here. If you don't mind, I would like to keep that on the low for now."

"Of course, how long you been down?"

"Just got here today."

"Oh okay, well I'm gonna let you grab something to eat. Don't forget to come back and see me now."

I nodded before giving him another hug and walking off to the table, meeting Una. As soon as I sat down across from her, she was deep into her phone. I cleared my throat gaining her attention. She lifted her head up before releasing a long sigh.

"What's wrong?"

"Nothing, my mama wanted me to go to Walmart and grab some stuff for the cookout Wednesday." she replied running her hands through her curly afro.

"I can grab it for you tomorrow. Just text me what you need and give me the money. Since Nana's going to a wedding tomorrow, I need something to do."

"Thank you, girl because I ain't feel like doing that."

"You never feel like doing nothing with your lazy ass."

She flicked me off before we shared a loud obnoxious laugh. After ordering our food, we sat at the table reminiscing about our childhood and how much we'd changed. For once in my life my anxiety seemed to feel non-existent. The rapid beating in my chest was slow and steady, and I was finally regaining my comfort back.

All of those emotions flew right out of the window when I looked up seeing my ex's mother, Judy, walk through the door.

Chapter 5: Skeletons

Samya

"Samya?" she asked removing her dark Gucci shades.

I swallowed the lump in my throat before wiping my sweaty palms on my pants. There I was literally standing face to face with the woman whose son I'd put behind bars for life. Una kicked me under the table to kick me out of the trance I was stuck in.

"Uh, hi." I replied, trying not to choke over my words.

"Oh my God! I thought you were dead or something. You vanished off the face of the earth and here I am finally seeing you." she smiled, bringing me into a tight hug and kissing my forehead.

"Yeah, I've been really busy."

"Well, I'm glad I bumped into you. I just got from the prison visiting my son. We talked about you the majority of the time. You're all he asks about."

Una saw the instant fear and worry in my eyes before she stood up and grabbed my arm.

"Well, you guys can catch up later. Mya and I gotta go check up on our Nana." Said Una, trying to pull me away from her. Before Una could pull me out, Judy grabbed my arm and held on tight.

"Just remember you're always gonna be a part of my family. Keep in touch." she smiled letting me go. Una pulled me out of the restaurant and to her car. We got inside and she pulled out of the parking lot pulling off.

"You okay?" she asked placing her hand over mine for comfort.

"Yeah, I'm fine. I just didn't expect her to pop up on me like that."

"Look, I already told you there's nothing to worry about. Cam can't do anything to you out here. He's in prison for life without parole. I don't know how many times I have to stress this."

"Don't do that. Don't act like you don't know what that man put me through. I don't want to be around anything that has a connection with him especially his damn mother."

"You know what, I don't feel like arguing with you right now. I see you still got that hard ass head of yours."

"And I see your ass don't know how to leave well enough alone."

The car ride was dead silent for a good ten minutes before Una sighed and looked over to me.

"I'm sorry. It's just I haven't been around you in years and this all feels so surreal to me right now. I never truly knew how fucked up this shit made you. I'm just happy you're finally home for a week."

"No, you're fine. It's just that I'm having trouble slowly letting people back in. I've been distant for so long because I'm just scared and I'm still trying to adjust to getting back to my old self." I replied staring off to the side.

"Well you could have always trusted me since diaper days, and you know that. I'm always gonna be here for you because I was always the pain in the ass, so you know I'm not going anywhere.

"I know." I laughed.

"So, when are you going to see your mom?"

"I guess I'll see her at the cookout."

"That'll work. You just gonna pop up like Houdini in front of the whole family?"

"Yup." I replied as if it was so simple.

Una and I spent the entire day shopping and catching up, until it was time for her to get ready to go out with Dezzy. As soon as she dropped me off, my Nana's gold Cadillac was sitting in the driveway. As soon as I went inside, the smell of Gumbo ran through my nostrils like a race. Walking into the kitchen she was humming the lyrics to Etta James' *At last* while stirring her pot.

"My lonely days are over." I sung loudly catching her off guard.

She turned around and all I could do was smile and stare at her. Her coil grey hair were now in curls bouncing off of her shoulders. I could tell she'd lost a little bit of hair due to her chemo, along with the pale color of her skin.

"Samya?" she asked squinting her eyes as if she couldn't believe I was standing in front of her.

"Yes." I replied, not even caring that my voice cracked.

I knew the tears were coming. I walked up to her and pulled her almost frail body into mine. I inhaled the scent of her vanilla perfume and clung onto her as if she was going somewhere. I was finally reunited with the woman who raised me and truly believed in me when I needed it the most. The woman who beat my ass whenever I down talked myself.

"Child, I know you not crying." she laughed, pulling back and wiping my tears with her thumb.

"Yes, I'm crying because I missed you." I sniffled before letting out a little laugh.

"I missed you too, child."

"So how are you feeling? You getting any better?" I asked walking behind her to the stove.

"I'm still kicking ain't I?" she laughed.

"Yes, you are but still, I worry about you. You tend to hide what your doctors say away from me and Una. We shouldn't have to call your doctor to find out the truth when I'm the one paying for your chemo, Nana."

"Look here. I'm a grown woman and I know how to handle my own. I've been doing it for seventy-three years now and I don't need my grandchild telling me about my health. I know you're scared but I'm fighting this battle, not you. Stop worrying about me. If it's my time, then God up there waiting on me and there's no need to interfere with his plans."

I looked down at my feet feeling like a little kid who'd gotten scolded. My Nana was always strong willed and didn't like when people pitied her. I wasn't even going to lie and say I wasn't nervous about my Nana's health. She'd recently stopped smoking cigarettes due to her being on chemo. She lifted my face up to hers before giving me a disappointed look.

"You over here worrying about me and here I am worrying about you. The Samya I raised never hung her head low. I'm real disappointed in you and I've been waiting the longest to tell you this to your face. How could you let somebody run you out of your home?"

"Nana there's more to the story."

"Mhm, and I expect to hear it all."

"You will."

"Good, now sit down, my gumbo almost done." she smiled pulling bowls from the cabinet.

I sat in the kitchen for two hours venting to my Nana about everything that happened to me when I'd left her to move to Houston. All the way throughout venting, I felt a huge weight being lifted off of my shoulders. I just felt I could only tell my Nana every little piece of my journey with ease because she was there for me. She held me as I cried full tears into her arms; I finally felt comforted. A feeling I'd been burning inside for since I'd left home. I finally felt like I could be at ease because I'd never truly told anyone in detail what happened to me.

After crying for up to an hour until I couldn't cry anymore, my Nana finally got me to calm down.

"God put us through trials and tribulations to test our strengths and power. I knew you were going to be strong the first day I held you in my arms. Baby you gotta get all of this bad energy off your back you hear?"

"I know." I sniffled wiping my eyes.

"I'm going to need you to take a shower and meet me in my bedroom before you go to bed. Soak and take a nice bath and relax, okay?"

I nodded before kissing her forehead and giving her one last hug, heading to my room. Digging in my suitcase, I pulled out a pair of Nike boy shorts and a white tank top. Heading into the bathroom across from my room, I started my bath before stripping out of my clothes. While the tub continued to rise with water, I stood in the mirror naked as the day I was born, looking at myself. My eyes were still red and puffy from all the crying I was doing not long ago. After venting I felt light and worry free; the feeling was all content to me.

After taking a bath, I got dressed and made my way to my Nana's room. I stopped at her cracked door inhaling the scent of shea butter and honey scented candles. Pushing the door open, the sound of the creaks made her pop her head up from her journal.

"How do you feel?" she asked adjusting the glasses on her face.

"A lot better." I smiled walking over and sitting next to her.

"Good, I told you." she replied closing her journal before I could get a good look at it.

"What do you be writing in there?"

"Thoughts, feelings, dreams, and accomplishments."

"You've been writing in journals since I was a little girl. You telling me that's all in there?"

"Yup. Looking back and reading my first journal entry to now, I can say I lived a good life. I had seven amazing kids, I own a bakery, I have grandkids and great-grandkids I lived to see, and I married the man of my dreams." she smiled, looking over at the photo of her and my grandad on the nightstand.

"I know you still miss him."

"Everyday." she smiled.

"So, what you called me in for?"

"To check up on you for number one. And number two, I got something to get rid of all that bad energy."

"Nana I thought you said you don't smoke weed."

"Don't play with me, I ain't talking about no damn weed." she replied giving me the side eye.

"My bad." I laughed.

"Sit on floor and close your eyes. You open them when I tell you to."

I nodded before sitting on the floor and closing my eyes. I heard the light switch click, indicating that she'd turned off the lights. My nostrils were now filled with the scent of sage. Feeling the presence of my Nana around me, I already knew what she was doing due to her being a spiritual person. I felt all the bad vibes and energy slowly leaving me; a feeling I hadn't felt before.

"Open your eyes."

I slowly opened my eyes seeing that she was clearing the bad energy from around her as well. Once she was finished, we meditated for an hour before I left her alone to go to sleep. Lying in bed looking at the ceiling, I smiled feeling a sense of security. Feeling that I could finally sleep and go an entire night without undergoing another nightmare. Looking over at the nightstand that read 12:00 AM, my eyes grew heavy and I didn't bother to fight my sleep like I'd found myself doing back in Houston.

I woke up to the sound of metal hitting together. Rubbing my eyes and letting out a groggy groan, I pulled the covers from over my body and placed my feet on the wooden floors. Grabbing a pair of socks from my suitcase, I slid them on before making my way out of the room and into the kitchen, where the noise was coming from. Stepping into the frame of the kitchen, I crossed my arms and raised my eyebrow once I saw a man standing at the door drilling nails into the wood.

"Yo!" I yelled over the sound of the power drill.

I scoffed in disbelief seeing he paid me no attention. I brought my attention to the clock on the wall that read 8:30 before running my hands through my hair. One thing I didn't play about was my sleep and I usually slept in till nine. Even though it was only thirty minutes of sleep left, I still was tired from the drive the day prior.

"I know you heard me!" I yelled, clapping my hands behind his head but still received no response.

Finally getting aggravated, I tapped his shoulder before he turned around pulling AirPods from his ears, that I didn't realize were in. He shoved his AirPods in his pocket before licking his lips and looking down at me.

"So, you decide to want to make noise at eight o'clock in the morning as if nobody sleeping in this neighborhood?" I said while giving him the side eye. I was beyond furious and I knew I had to start my work later running off of a few hours of sleep.

"Never knew Mrs. Gale had a roommate move in." He replied making my heart drop to my ass.

I didn't know if it was the lack of sexual affection I was getting, but just the baritone modulation of his voice made a puddle form in my shorts. Clearing my throat, I removed my eyes from his broad muscular shoulders and got my head straight.

"I'm her granddaughter, not a roommate. I used to live here."

"Oh, my bad I ain't know." He replied putting down his tools and wiping his hands on his sweats.

"Well, now you do. Can you be a little more, quiet I was hoping to get some more sleep before I start getting busy later."

"Of course, my apologies."

"Okay, thanks." I replied about to walk back into my room.

"Damn, no introduction." He chuckled shaking his head.

"Excuse me?"

"I mean I don't know where you from but around here, we introduce ourselves. I'm Jay, nice to meet you. So, this is the part where you give me your name."

"Goodbye, Jay." I replied before walking off rolling my eyes.

I shook my head before going back in my room and closing my door. Pulling out my MacBook, I decided to get to work early. Even though I worked at the salon part time, I had my own business. I was a graphic designer and sold art pieces from my personal website. Logging into my website, I saw almost two hundred orders that were put in. Running my hands through my hair, I opened my Spotify and attempted to get most of my work done. It wasn't even a full thirty minutes before there was a knock on my door. Before I could throw a repulsive response thinking it was the guy who was working on the door, Una burst through with an IHOP bag.

"Hey cousin!" She smiled plopping down on my bed and looking into my laptop.

"Hey. What you doing here?"

"Coming to see you before I go to work."

"Well as you can see, I'm working myself."

"I see that now. Well I bought you some IHOP, hopefully you still like blueberry pancakes."

"I do."

"Good because that's all you got." She laughed.

"Thanks, I was gonna grab something later on, but you saved me a trip."

"You're welcome, but did you meet Jay?" She asked wiggling her eyebrow.

"Yes, I met the man who disturbed my damn slumber."

"That is not a man, that is a God." She replied sticking her tongue out.

"He aight."

"You know what, I think you gay. You gotta like pussy or something because you never talk about a man. Even when you were in Houston our conversations were always about how you don't need a man."

"I'm straight, so don't play me. I'm just focused on my self-care right now and my job."

"Wow, okay, whatever floats your boat. I'm about to hit

this road, don't forget to go to Walmart for me. I already cash app you the money."

"Alright, I got you."

She gave me a hug before making her way out of the house. After finishing most of my orders, which took two hours, I took a quick shower and got dressed for the day. Grabbing my Louis Voution purse, I made my way out of my room feeling relieved that I didn't see Jay in sight. I wasn't really in the mood to play meet and greet. I knew I was giving off the vibe that I was being a bougie, stuck up bitch but in all actuality, it was in my character. I was never a vocal or social person when it came to people. That trait of mine was also one of the things that pushed people away. I knew the type of person I was when it came to men, or anybody in general.

Making my way out of the door, I raised my eyebrow in curiosity on why Jay was sitting on the porch with two other guys, laughing it up as if it were his property. As soon as I opened the screen door, all eyes were on me. My eyes began to roam Jay's body once again. His smooth chocolate skin tone could be seen through the plain white T-shirt he had on.

"So, we just gonna act like people don't live here and block the porch, right?" I said sarcastically with my arms crossed, making my attitude evident.

Jay laughed before the other two guys joined in. I didn't find anything funny. They then presumed to go back to their conversation.

"So, I guess imma fucking ghost." I said simply before bumping pass them rolling my eyes, until Jay gripped my arm, causing me to reach for my can of mace. I was prepared to burn the nigga's eyes out of the sockets.

"Yo, imma need you to calm that down. Ms.Gale know we always here in the mornings. That lady like a grandmother to me too. I'm here almost every morning."

"Well that's gonna have to change because for one, you were loud as fuck this morning and for two, when I plan on leaving the house, I don't plan on being ambushed."

He simply chuckled before stepping to the side to let me go, as his friend jumped in my face with a cocky smile. Rolling my eyes once more, I showed him my can of mace and he stepped back.

"Aight, before you try and blind a nigga let me give you my name."

"I don't want your name and I'm not giving out mine." I replied trying to step around him, but he stepped in my direction.

"Damn she rude ain't she? Y'all must don't do introductions where you from."

"That's what I said." Mumbled Jay.

"Are you done or are you finished wasting my time?"

"Damn baby girl I ain't-"

"Don't call me that, my name ain't, baby girl." I replied quickly getting uncomfortable just from being called that.

"Man, Ace leave that damn girl alone. My bad about my brother, I'm Jace by the way." Said the other guy pulling Ace from in front of me.

"Nice to meet you." I simply replied giving a head nod before walking off towards my car and speeding out of the driveway.

Chapter 6: Balance

Jayceon

"I'd be done slap the shit outta ol girl." Scoffed Ace pulling his phone from his pocket.

"You only saying that cause she don't want yo ol bean head ass." Jace replied sucking his teeth.

"Baby girl want me, she just don't know it yet."

"Nigga where you get that clue from?" I asked with a raised brow.

"The way she looked at me. Shawty want a nigga, she probably got a bitch made nigga anyway, that's probably why she acting so stuck up."

"So, you mad that she dusted yo ass or the fact that she might got a nigga?" I asked still not understanding Ace's logic.

Ace and Jace were brothers from Compton. Ace was the youngest being twenty-four while Jace was twenty. Out of both of them, Ace was the childish brother who always held a don't give a fuck attitude. Where Jace on the other hand, was the charmer and the responsible one of the two. You would have thought the two were twins by their names and their looks.

"First and foremost, if she got a nigga, he ain't me."

"That girl don't want you, man." Jace and I said in unison.

"Yeah right. I bet the nigga broke lil baby's heart that's why she like that. But she gonna find out I'm different. I bet her old nigga took her to McDonald's but me, imma take her to Wendy's; she can get a better deal with a four for four." He smiled rubbing his hands together.

Jace sucked his teeth before popping Ace upside the head. Fishing in my pocket for my keys, I stood up and headed towards my Range Rover.

"Where the hell you going, nigga?" asked Jace getting up from his spot on the porch.

"I gotta meet Sabrina people at that French Restaurant on Ferry."

"Aw shit, dinner with Mrs. Bougie and Mr. Stuck up." Ace laughed before shaking his head.

"They not bougie."

"Then what the fuck they is then?"

"I don't know but they are not bougie."

"Yeah, aight. Your ass better be on the court with us tomorrow after you finish playing Mr. Kiss ass."

I shooed them off before getting into my car and driving on the other side of town to meet up with my wife, Sabrina. Rubbing one hand across my face while the other gripped the wheel, I was prepared to hear the bullshit that was going to leave her parent's mouth. As bad as I didn't want to admit it in front of my boys, Sabrina's parents were in fact bougie as hell. Shit, they were the upper-class Huxtables. Her mother, Leane, was a doctor and her dad, James, was a judge. Shit, damn near the entire family was successful and never had to scrape up change to make a dollar.

Pulling into my driveway, I killed the engine and got out going inside. As soon as I opened the door, my pit bull terrier,

King, ran towards me with his tongue hanging from his mouth. I smiled before squatting down and fluffing his ears.

"Baby it's almost time to go, what are you wearing?" said Sabrina coming from the kitchen, dressed in a Tommy Hilfiger dress and a pair of gold Tom Ford padlock heels.

"I'm wearing clothes, what the hell you wearing?"

"I really don't feel like this, you know how my dad gets whenever you dress like that."

"You fucking serious right now, Brina?" I scoffed looking down at my sweats and Nike T. I didn't even want to meet up with her damn parents anyway and this was a prime example why. She loved to front and make me look like somebody I wasn't whenever we were around them.

"Yes, I picked out your suit, it's on the bed."

"Who the fuck wearing a suit when it's hot as hell outside."

"You! Now put it on before I get pissed off, we already about to be late."

I bit my tongue because I already knew it was going to start an argument that I didn't have time for. Going towards my room, I shook my head seeing the Tom Ford suit laid out on the bed. Quickly throwing on the suit, I met Sabrina downstairs where she was looking down on her phone.

"You ready?" I asked grabbing my keys from the coffee table.

"Yeah, and grab both of those bags for me." she replied pointing at the two gift bags on the table.

I grabbed the bags and made my way to the door. After opening the door for her, I got inside and made my way to the restaurant. As soon as I saw Sabrina's parent's silver Rolls Royce, I parked beside it before killing the engine.

"I don't see the reason for this damn tight ass suit." I mumbled.

"It's not that tight, babe, now come on."

I sighed, getting out of the car and making my way to her side of the door, helping her out. Grabbing her hand, we walked through the double doors of the restaurant.

"Yes, reservations for Smith." said Sabrina to the host.

"Of course, right this way." she replied giving me a polite smile.

I returned the gesture getting ready to follow her, but Sabrina grabbed my hand and brushed past her. I already knew she was going to bring up how I should have never smiled back, or how I sat there and practically flirted with another girl in her face. We made our way to the round table where her parents sat in a secluded area. As soon as she saw her parents, she let go of my hand and embraced both of them into a hug. As soon as she let them go, her dad approached me before extending his hand. I gave him a firm grip, shaking his hand before letting go and giving him a genuine smile.

"Jayceon, how have you been?" he asked.

I knew he was just putting up a front like he usually did when we got together. He'd already made it perfectly clear that I wasn't good enough for his daughter. I ran my own youth center, co-owned my family's soul food restaurant, and I was a therapist. I assumed my background overshadowed my Bachelor's Degree in psychology and business.

"I've been well. You?"

"Splendid."

"That's good to know."

"Jayceon, honey I haven't seen you in months." said Sabrina's mother pulling me into a hug.

"Same, Ms. Leane, how you been?"

"I've been great."

"That's good."

"Okay, everybody sit down I called you all here for a reason." Said Sabrina, grabbing both gift bags and sitting down.

"So Jayceon, how is that Doctoral Degree coming along?" asked James, already knowing I was going back to school.

"I'm not going back to school."

"And why is that? Can't afford it? I mean I can pay-."

"I'm perfectly fine with what I'm doing now, thank you for your of-."

"I have no issue providing for you. I provide for my family all the time."

"I provide for myself."

"You sure about that?"

"Okay enough, James." said Leane, placing her hand over his. Sabrina squeezed my hand under the table sensing my anger.

"Can I talk please. I could have sworn I called this lunch together for a good reason."

"Did you know your husband was in prison for three years?" said James passing an envelope to Sabrina.

"James!" said Leane with a shocked expression.

"Daddy I-." Sabrina was about to speak before he interrupted her.

"No, I don't think it's okay for my daughter to be married to an ex-con. Shit, he probably was the reason his own damn son got killed."

The vain in my head began to twitch as I stood up getting ready to swing on his ass for speaking on my child. For even thinking I had anything to do with my child's passing.

"Go ahead, hit me so I can max your ass straight to prison." he said with his arms crossed unphased.

He thought just because he was a judge his ass couldn't be touched but I was going show his ass. Sabrina grabbed ahold of me before giving her father a look of disapproval.

"He's a damn murderer." said William throwing his hands in the air.

"Don't speak on shit you don't know about."

"That's enough! Look, I thought today was going to be peaceful because we haven't seen each other in months. Daddy this is my husband, he's the father of my kids."

"Kids?" Leane asked with a raised eyebrow.

"Yes, kids. I brought everyone here to announce that I'm pregnant."

I looked down at her with a smile as bright as the sun. All the anger her father got out of me went out of the window after hearing what just came out of her mouth. I was in utter shock because when I'd met Sabrina, she could never have kids. Our son was a miracle baby and she nearly died giving birth to him. I was ecstatic hearing the news because I'd been wanting another baby for the longest. Walking past my son's room everyday knowing it was empty weighed down in my heart heavy. I didn't even realize I was crying until Sabrina wiped my tears away with her thumb. James clenched his jaw while Leane walked over to bring Sabrina and I into a tight hug.

"Open these." said Sabrina giving me and her mother the bags.

I opened it and reached inside, pulling out a white onesie that read, *See you in 9 months dad.* I laughed before pulling Sabrina into my arms and pecking her lips. One thing I could say about my wife was she never switched up on me, even when it came to her parents. Then and now she may try to put on a front in their presence, but she always stood by me.

"I love you." she smiled.

"I love you too."

I smiled watching Leane open the bag and pulling out the other onesie. James stood up and kissed Sabrina's forehead before going towards the door.

"I'm going to talk to him." said Leane walking towards the direction James had gone.

"I'm sorry about him, he always acts like this and I should have never planned this without giving you a heads up."

"Baby, it's fine, all that matters is our baby right now. I don't give a damn about what he thinks."

"I know you don't, but I do."

"Don't let it stress you out. I'll find a day to where me and him can have a one on one."

"I'd really appreciate that."

"I know you would. I wanna apologize, I should have never let him get me out of character."

"It's my father, he always does that."

"Still, I-."

"You nothing. Don't let it happen again, okay? Now let's order our food." She interrupted kissing my cheek."

Jalisa

"That's on my mama, yeah that on the hood. You don't want no problems; I wish a bitch would." I sung while typing on my MacBook.

"How I look?" asked my friend, Infinity, coming from my walk-in closet.

"Like a damn thief. Why do you have on my halter top?" I asked closing my laptop.

"Because I don't have shit to wear to BJ's party, so I raided your closet."

"Ew, the ratchetivity." I laughed.

"Don't play me."

"I'm not playing you. It's just you go to every damn party he throws! I invited you over to chill with me since my sister was out of town for the week."

"And I told you I would chill with you but not every day. Come on, just come to the party with me."

"Nope, you know I don't do parties."

"And I wanna change that."

"My mind won't change. Especially since it's one of BJ's parties."

"What's wrong with BJ's parties?"

"Didn't someone get shot twice at his party."

"That was because his security was ass, duh."

"You know what, I said no. Go have fun, I'll get Ash to come and keep me company."

"Ash is coming with me too, so."

"I'll stay home, I have a book to write." I replied opening my MacBook again.

"You don't get paid for writing books, so therefore close your laptop and come shake some ass with me tonight."

"Well, I have to keep writing so I can earn this scholarship. Unlike y'all, I'd like to go to college."

"I should be offended but I'm not. Look your sister probably in Atlanta doing some Hot Girl shit. You need to loosen up."

"Fine, I'll go. Just for two hours and I'm leaving."

"That's fine."

"Okay, and I'm driving because when I say I'm ready to go, I mean it."

"That's fine too, as long as you come."

"Okay."

"And the theme is nineties kickback."

"I see that." I replied looking at her complete outfit.

Getting out of bed, I went to my closet and put on something that made me resemble Aaliyah the best I could. Once I was ready, I grabbed the keys to my Jeep and locked up the house. Getting in the car, Infinity put the address into the GPS. It took us a good fifteen minutes before we arrived outside of BJ's party, where cars lined the block. It took us a good five minutes before we could find a place to park. Getting out, the entire vibe felt off to me. I didn't know if it was because I wasn't a social person and this scene was out of my comfort zone, or if it was because Samya was gone and if anything happened, she was miles away.

"Girl if you don't loosen the fuck up!" said Infinity throwing her arms over my shoulder.

"I am, now let's go inside before I turn around."

She grabbed my hand as we pushed through crowd of people to go inside. The smell of weed and alcohol clouded the closer we got inside. Montell Jordan's *This is How we Do It* blasted through the speakers of the house while everyone danced and drank.

"Yo BJ." said Infinity calling him over.

"Why you calling that boy over here?" I asked not in the mood to talk to anyone. I don't even know why my antisocial ass agreed to come in the first place.

This was a prime example on why I didn't like going out. Talking to people made me uncomfortable. Living like an introvert took a toll on me. BJ walked over with a big smile showing his grill.

"Infinity, wassup baby?" he greeted pulling her into a hug. I rolled my eyes watching Infinity, Ash, and a few of the other girls, gawk over him.

"Who this?" he asked eyeing me up and down.

"You know me, I'm Jalisa the girl you cheated off of in Calculus."

"Oh yeah, pretty young thang from calculus. How could I forget about you?"

"I chose for you not to remember me."

"Damn it's like that?"

"Yup."

"This your first time coming to one of my parties?"

"You can say that."

"Say word! Damn well you wanna dance?"

"Nah, I'm fine."

"You sure?"

"Yeah, I'm gucci."

"Aight, well if you want to later, just holla if you need me."

I rolled my eyes before giving him a head nod and walking off with Infinity and Ash on my trail.

"Bitch you must be on crack! Did you just decline BJ?" said Ash.

"Yes, I did decline him. Unlike y'all I don't gawk over prison records and guys with no diploma."

"You know what, I had enough of your shit, Lisa, like really?" said Infinity crossing her arms.

"Whatsoever do you mean?"

"You know exactly what the fuck I mean. I'm tired of you fucking dogging me out like seriously, that shit get old. The next time you say some slick shit thinking you better than somebody I'ma knock your fucking head off your shoulders."

"Well bitch, do it then! This is my mouth; I say what the fuck I want to. Don't get fucked up in front of all these people."

"Alright y'all, calm that shit down." said Ashley stepping in between us.

"Nah, the only reason I'm here is because of her ass. She know this ain't my fucking scene. She pushed me to fucking come here already knowing how the fuck I was going to act. What she expect me to fucking do throw back shots and fuck some random upstairs like she do?"

Infinity tried to walk up on me, but Ashley pulled her back. I grabbed my keys from my pocket before turning my back.

"That's why yo own fuckin crack head ass mama ain't want you bitch! With yo skank ass sister, that's why that bitch fucked her way to get most of the shit she got!" yelled Infinity.

I turned around watching everybody go quiet and a few

even laughed with her. Walking past the table and grabbing the Grey Goose bottle, I ran up on her from behind and bashed her in her head, watching her stumble forward and fall on the floor. My blood was boiling to the point where I was about to explode like a damn volcano. I confided in Infinity and Ashley with my life story because we were friends for years. We were complete opposites, but we were best friends. They preferred to party and do fuck shit where when it came to me, I was focused on my future and building myself.

I walked towards her and ripped my shirt off of her unconscious body, receiving shocked expressions from everybody seeing me get out of character. I didn't even know I had tears streaming from my eyes before I started hyperventilating. Someone grabbed me pulling me away from all of the attention. I didn't even know I was halfway down the road from the house before the stranger got into my face grabbing ahold of me.

"Are you good?" he asked trying to calm me down.

"I'm okay."

"No, you're not, it doesn't look like it."

"Look, I said I'm fine!"

"I'm just trying to make sure you are before you head out and end up in a damn tree."

"I said I'm okay." I replied, not even noticing that I was crying into his chest. I knew I was pissed and in need of my medication, because It wasn't like me to let a complete stranger comfort me. I felt as if I was about to go to jail with the criminal thoughts that ran through my head. My ADHD was kicking in full gear and I felt it coming full force.

Chapter 7: Who Am I

Samya

"Girl you ready?" asked Una while picking out her afro.

"Yeah, I'm ready. I'm just trying to get in touch with Jalisa. She hasn't called me this morning yet." I replied looking down at my call log.

"Jalisa is fine, her ass probably in that bed knocked out."

"Una, it's twelve in the afternoon. She's always up at this time."

"Look, she'll call, trust me."

"I hope." I sighed, still feeling bad that she had no clue where I was. I knew she was going to be pissed off since she hadn't seen anyone since she was younger. I didn't even know if she remembered half of our family because it had been so long.

"Come on, we gotta head out before my mama start blowing me up. She already up my ass about not telling her that you were here."

"Why you in such a rush? The cookout is literally three houses down."

"Yeah and you already know Aunt Teema like to feed the entire damn neighborhood."

"Yeah, I know." I laughed getting ready to walk out the door, but she grabbed me and pulled me by the mirror.

"Uh uh, I ain't seen yo ass in years. This is a kodak moment, let's take a picture. Only Lord knows how long it'll be until I see you again when you leave." she smiled posing in front of the mirror and holding up her phone.

"You better not post it either." I said through a gritted smile, waiting for her to snap the picture.

"I'm not, since your ass is undercover."

After she'd snapped the picture on her phone, we made our way out the front door and to my aunt's house. For some reason I was nervous. I looked down at my Yeezy sneakers, plain denim jeans, and white Louis Vuitton crop top. I tried to dress as plain and simple as I could, not trying to give off the wrong impression. Una must have sensed my bad nerves because she squeezed my hand in comfort as we got closer to the house. I felt as if I was meeting a bunch of strangers the closer we'd gotten.

"You got this, it's just family. The worst thing they can do is talk shit." said Una squeezing my hand tighter.

"Yeah I know."

As soon as we stepped foot in the yard eyes were all on me, as if I was this mysterious creature.

"Is that my damn niece, Samya?" said my uncle Willie coming up to me with a shocked expression on his face with a red plastic cup in his hand.

"It's me." I laughed noticing he hadn't changed one bit. His beard was still cut to his liking and by the looks of the red cup in his hand, he was still an alcoholic.

"Either I'm drunk from one sip, or my niece is really standing in front of me." he said while circling me.

"I said it's me, Uncle Willie." I laughed.

"I'll be damn!" he said before pulling me into a hug. I felt like a little kid again. The same little girl that would get off the bus and run to hug him. The same little girl who would get into trouble and run to him for protection. I didn't know if I missed my Nana, Una, or him the most.

"I missed you too." I laughed.

"What you doin here? Where's little Lisa?" he asked pulling away from the hug and looking down the road.

"I'm here visiting for a week. And Jalisa is back at home preparing herself for college."

"Oh okay, well I'm happy to see you. Last time I saw you, you was this high." he said holding his hand up to his chest.

"I know."

"Well dang, I'm here to Uncle Willie." said Una, jumping in front of me with a smile as big as the sun.

"I see yo big ass apple head, I wish I didn't. Every time you see me you want something." He said making me laugh. Una gave him a peeved expression.

"Since you wanna be funny. Let me borrow twenty dollars for gas." she said trying to reach for his pockets.

"You better go somewhere before I stump a mud hole in ya ass, now!" he said walking away from her.

"You always messing with him." I laughed.

"I knew that laugh sounded familiar," said my Aunt Sasha coming up through the crowd. You couldn't miss my aunt Sasha even if you were a blind man. She was as curvaceous as a coke bottle; shit she was curvier than that. She always rocked a black, short haircut and when she was feeling fancy, she sported blonde.

"Hey aunt Sasha." I smiled.

"Don't hey Aunt Sasha me, you can't hang up on me now that I'm in your face, heffa! As bad as I want to beat you down,

I've missed you too much." she replied pulling me into a hug and squeezing me tight, as if I would blow away if she'd let me go.

"Ma, you don't hug me like that." said Una with crossed arms.

"Because I don't like you."

I laughed watching both of them bicker back and forth, missing them already. After reminiscing with almost my entire family, I felt as if I could finally hold onto the piece of sanity and sobriety I had left. The only people I didn't want to bump into, would be my mother and stepfather. Ever since I'd arrived, they weren't in sight and to be honest, I wasn't mentally prepared to talk to her yet. I was actually happy that she was nowhere in sight.

I sat in the kitchen with Una and the rest of my cousin playing Uno.

"Nah nigga, you can't make me draw twelve!" said my cousin Lamar.

"Watch me." said Una preparing to lay her cards on the table.

"Do it and I'll air this bitch out!"

"Not in my house you won't!" said my aunt Teema coming up behind us.

We all shared a laugh before Una placed her cards on the table, making Lamar throw his cards on the table and walk off.

"Niece your mama here." said my Aunt Sasha catching me off guard.

"Y'all I'll be back, I'm gonna go to the bathroom."

I quickly placed my cards on the table and jogged up the stairs, heading towards my aunt's bedroom. Placing my back against the door, I calmed my nerves with my eyes closed.

"Okay Mya, you got this. This is what you're down here

for." I said to myself pacing back and forth.

"You good lil Ms. Attitude?" said Jayceon, coming from the bathroom conjoined to the room.

"What are you doing here?" I asked not in the mood for the antics him and his friends pulled earlier.

"I was invited, they consider me a family friend."

"What are you doing in her personal bathroom? She never lets anybody come in here."

"I fixed up some stuff for her."

"So, you're some type of handyman?" I asked with a raised brow.

"That's not my profession but my pops used to be one and taught me the ropes."

"Hm, I guess."

"So, what you in here hiding for. You asking me twenty-one questions, so I'm gonna ask you one."

"I'm in here trying to catch a break."

"From what?" he asked, raising his brow in confusion like I'd done earlier.

"That's none of your business."

As soon as I heard footsteps coming up the stairs along with my name being called, I ran to my aunt's closet and hid. I watched through the crack of the door as my aunt Sasha swung the door open looking around.

"Jay, you seen my niece Samya?"

I watched as he eyed the closet before he cleared his throat, shaking his head no. My aunt sighed before closing the door and heading back downstairs. I opened the door and he looked at me before laughing.

"Samya?" Hm, I like that."

"Real funny."

"What you done did for them to be hunting you down?" he asked leaning on the wall.

"I told you it's none of your business."

"I will rat yo ass out right now. Your aunt already told me your name."

I looked at him daring him to do it. As soon as he yelled my aunt Sasha's name, I ran and tackled him to the bed, holding my hand over his mouth. I glanced over at the door hoping no one heard him.

"Fine, I'll tell you, just shut the fuck up!" I said through gritted teeth.

"Good, now can you get off me?" he replied looking at the position we were in. I climbed from off of him and removed my hand from his mouth, before sitting down beside him.

"I'm ready?" he asked with a wide smile as if I had some big news to share.

"I'm hiding from a family member."

"Obviously I know that. Why though?"

"I'm hiding from my mother."

"Why?"

"I haven't seen her in years. This is my first week back here and ever since I've gotten here, I feel as if I've been walking on eggshells. I've been so nervous and scared thinking about how everyone would react to me and everything has been good so far. But my mom, we left on bad terms."

"It can't be that hard."

"Trust me, I love my mama and all, but I'm scared to face her thinking she's going to be the same old person I left behind."

"You'll never know if she's the same person if you don't approach her."

"I'm not mentally prepared to face her right now and that's what my family won't understand. Half the time, I don't even know who I am." I replied placing my face in my palms.

"When was the last time you had fun?" he asked grabbing ahold of my hand.

"What?"

"When was the last time you had fun? The last time you enjoyed yourself?"

"Back at home all I did was raise my sister and work. I don't have time for fun."

"And that's the thing. You spend so much time trying to prepare yourself for shit, that you don't genuinely know how it feels to let go and walk through the fire without fearing the outcome."

"What are you some type of therapist or something?"

"You could say that." he smiled standing up and extending his hand.

"I'm not going out there."

"I know, now come on."

I placed my hand in his before he lead me to the bathroom window. Opening it, he looked at me to go first. I looked at him as if he'd lost his mind.

"I'm not going through no damn window."

"Or you can walk through them doors and meet me outside."

I looked towards the door before looking at the window. "Come on man." I pouted.

"You got this."

"I hope so." I replied climbing out the window and climbing down the side of the house. After I made it down, he closed the window and climbed down as well.

"Come on."

"Where are you taking me?"

"Don't worry about that."

"You're a complete stranger to me, trust me I'm gonna worry about it."

"You just confided in me a few minutes ago."

"Because you threatened me, technically."

"Trust me, I'm not gonna murder you if that's what you thinking."

"I hope not."

I followed him to his car before we got in and he drove off to God knows where. I looked in the rearview mirror watching the house disappear from eye view.

"You good?"

"Yeah."

"I know you not hungry from all that damn food they had in there earlier."

"I'm not."

"Good, now I don't have to feed you."

"Mhm, whatever so where are we going?"

"To Sky Zone."

"I haven't been there in while. My big ass ain't finna jump on a trampoline."

"Yes, you are."

"No, I'm not. I'm too big for that." I laughed.

"No, you're not, you look perfectly fine to me. I like how you look."

"Whatever."

"I'm gonna assume you don't know how to take a compliment."

"Why do you assume that?"

"Because of your nonchalant ass response."

"Hm, maybe you're right, maybe you're wrong."

"Are you always this upfront when somebody's trying to be nice to you."

"I don't believe in people being genuinely nice. At the end of the day someone is going to want something out of somebody."

"That's a fucked-up way to live, thinking that."

"Well not all of us had a good life."

"Just looking at me, you think I lived a good life?"

"Yeah."

"Well you need to stop trying to read people because your assumption is wrong."

"Yeah right, what possibly could you have gone through."

"I prefer not to say."

"Uh uh, you were so quick to pressure me about my lil life story so I wanna know about you."

"Alright, I lost someone special to me. That's just one thing you need to know."

"I'm sorry to hear that." I replied automatically feeling bad just for prying.

"Nah, it's fine I've learned to talk about it."

"I wish I had strength like that."

"What's stopping you from getting it."

"The fear of losing myself."

"You can never lose yourself if you know who you truly are." he replied pulling into the parking lot. "Do you know who you are?" he then asked killing the engine and looking over at me.

"I'm still trying to figure that part out."

"You got your whole life to do so. Why not start now?"

"You're right." I smiled.

We got out of the car and made our way inside. After paying, Jayceon and I spent hours together talking and having fun. I couldn't believe I was finally getting what I had to say off of my chest to a complete stranger. I mean, confiding in my Nana was something I did easily, but with somebody I barely knew, this was different. For years, I'd talked to specialist and close friends about my troubles and they couldn't seem to find the right things to say to me but with him, he only knew bits and pieces of my story and I felt as if I was finally being understood. Not to mention the advice I was receiving from him actually taught me something. The thing that frightened me somewhat, was that I felt as if I knew him or as if we'd met before. That was what drew me to confide in him. The thing was, I couldn't put my finger on it. His presence didn't feel fully new to me.

Jay and I laid on the trampoline looking up at the window ceiling, watching the clouds roll in.

"Do you always take strangers out to Sky Zone and provide therapeutic advice."

"No, you're actually the first."

"Hm, I don't know how to feel about that." I laughed.

"You know your laugh and smile is contagious right?"

"How so?"

"It's just beautiful. I mean, my first time meeting you, you were ready to beat my ass. Why do you do that?"

"Do what?"

"Give people a hard time."

"I don't give people a hard time." I replied sitting up, side eyeing him.

"Yes, you do."

"No, I don't."

"Yeah right."

"Mhm, well I have a question of my own. How do you cope when you're n a bad head space?"

"A while back I nearly ended my own life. Then somebody gave me advice like I'm giving you."

"And what did this person say?"

"Somebody has to be there for the boulder when it cracks."

As soon as that sentence left his mouth, memories began to roll in like a Polaroid. Before I could say anything, his ringing phone interrupted us. After his quick conversation, he shoved his phone back into his pocket before helping me stand up.

"I gotta get to my wife. You want me to drop you off back to Teema's or your grandmother's place?"

"Uh, my grandmother's place is fine."

"I gotta head by my center real fast is that cool with you?"

"I'll catch an Uber."

"Nah, I can drop you off and then handle my busi-."

"I said I'll take an Uber. Thanks, this was fun while it lasted." I fake smiled before grabbing my shoes and walking out.

I made my way across the street to Chick Fil A and called an Uber. Sitting down near the window, I looked across the street to see Jayceon was gone. I scoffed before my attention landed on someone who looked like Seven. As soon as he turned around, I stood up and walked over after seeing what I'd saw.

"Are you fucking serious?!" I yelled jacking him up and pulling him to the side. He held a shocked expression as if he was surprised to see me there.

"The fuck are you doin here?"

"Visiting fucking family. What the fuck are you doing out here selling drugs?"

"That's none of your fucking business! You need to head back to Houston and stay out of what the fuck I got going on."

"I can't believe your ass right now! Are you fucking stupid or slow?"

"Not all of us got big fancy degrees, big sis. You gotta get it how you live. Unless you wanna lend your poor ghetto lil brother a thousand dollars."

"I'm not giving you shit."

"I figured. Now if you not gonna buy a rock, get the fuck outta my face." He replied walking off, but I grabbed his arm.

"If I give you a thousand dollars will you stop slanging?"

"I ain't gonna make no promises."

"Seven please, I'm begging you. I don't want you going down this path."

"Let me guess, you want me to be like Jalisa? I'm sorry, big sis, but I'm not finna be a kiss ass. I ain't Harvard material like she is."

"Look, are you gonna stop slanging? Answer the question!"

"I'll stop."

"Okay, I'll wire it to you."

"What's wrong? Don't trust me with your bank card."

"I said, I'll wire it to you. Now get home."

"You ain't my damn mama, just send me the money aight." He replied walking off, leaving me in the rain.

Chapter 8: Don't Judge Me

Samya

"Bitch he did what?" asked Una after I explained for the thousandth time.

"Remember the guy I told you about, when I first started stripping?"

"Yeah, mister make it rain on a bitch!"

"I think it was Jayceon."

"How you think it's him? I mean how do you even remember."

"Because I told him the same shit, he told me. The same shit my dad used to tell me."

"I'm not understanding this."

"Of course, you're not going to understand it. I just don't want to end up wrong."

"You probably are wrong. I mean, I don't know."

"Okay, Una." I replied just dropping the subject, feeling as if she wasn't listening to me.

"Don't do that."

"Do what?"

"Shut me out, you've been my cousin long enough for me to know when you're shutting me out."

"Because you're not listening to me."

"I am listening to you."

"No, you're not."

"Okay, Mya. What makes you think it's him other than what he told you?"

"I already said I don't know. I mean, I don't wanna walk up to him and be like, *hey remember me from six years ago at the strip club in Houston?* That would be weird as fuck if I'm wrong."

"You would never know if you don't ask. Or you could simply leave it alone."

"If you say so." I huffed, getting up and putting on my jacket.

"Where are you going?"

"To meet up with Seven."

"What his lil bad ass done did now?"

"Look, I'll catch you up later; it's a long story."

"Good God! Do you want me to come with you in case his hotheaded ass wanna get buck. Because I'll knock the dog shit outta his high yellow ass. See, you scared to put your hands on him but me, baby I'm different."

"No, you're not going to put your hands on him. I haven't had a close relationship with Seven in years and beating his ass ain't gonna help my case."

"Well he needs his ass beat. Walking around like the fucking world owe his ass something."

"I know, but just give him some time."

"I'm trying." she replied taking a deep breath. Una knew Seven talked shit every chance he got, and she knew how deep he could go in on somebody.

"I'll see you later, Una."

"Yea aight." she replied plugging her headphones in and lying back down in her bed.

Grabbing my keys, I made my way out the door and to my car. Getting inside, I drove straight to the address Seven gave me. I found myself passing by the classy apartment complexes, going deeper into the ghetto. I stopped further down the sidewalk once I noticed Seven smoking a cigarette, walking down the sidewalk with a few other guys. Driving up slowly by him and rolling my window down, he noticed me and rolled his eyes, before stopping in his tracks.

"So?" he said with his hands in his pocket, looking at me with his head to the side.

"Are you getting in, we need to sit down and talk."

"Meet me at mom's place."

"You know I'm not going there, Seven."

"Still running away like a lil bitch? I knew you ain't changed. Just because you took a drive here don't make shit any better."

"I'm tired of you talking to me like I'm your fucking child, Seven! I'm your fucking big sister, so get your ass in this car!" I yelled putting my car in park and getting out. His friends laughed in amusement as he looked at me like he was going to explode.

"I ain't going no damn where. Get your ass on, now."

"We were supposed to meet up and talk, and you being immature as fuck!"

"We talking now, ain't we?"

"You know what, fuck this, I'm done!" I yelled getting back in my car.

"That's right, get your ass in your car and run like you always do."

"If something happens to your dumb ass, don't call me."

"Bitch I was never gonna call you! I ain't call you then so why the fuck would I call you now?!" he yelled back. I knew he was as pissed off as I was, due to the vein twitching in his forehead.

"I fucking hate you!"

"I hate yo ass too! You were never my fucking sister so don't start now!"

I pulled off wiping my tears with the sleeve of my sweater. I wasn't gonna lie and say what he'd said didn't hurt me deep down to the core, because it did. He was right, why was I there now if I wasn't there for him then. Sniffling, I took a deep breath before calling Jalisa. I felt a sense of relief wave over me when she answered the phone.

"Hey."

"Hi." I smiled just from hearing her voice.

"What you calling for? Would have thought you was gonna be on your Hot Girl shit." she laughed.

"Nah, not without you."

"Aw, I feel the love. How's your trip though?"

"Could be better, I'm just ready to come home."

"Then come home, I miss you anyway."

"Yeah, I wish it was that easy. I promised that I would stay for a week and that's what I'm going to do. I thought you had Infinity keeping you company."

"Girl, I gotta tell you about that. I dragged that hoe!"

"Oh my God! What happened?"

"I'll give you details later but right now, I have to get ready to go to the animal shelter."

"Volunteer hours?"

"Yeah, you already know."

"That's my girl. I'm proud of you."

"I'm proud of myself too." she laughed.

"Alright, I'm gonna let you go. Love you and call me when you get done."

"Alright love you too, sis."

I clicked off before pulling into the parking lot of the bar. Getting out, I went inside and found a seat at the empty bar. It was a Monday morning and people were barely there. The bartender approached me with a genuine smile.

"What can I get you?" he asked.

"A shot of Tequila."

"This early?"

"I said a shot of Tequila, please." I repeated myself running my hands through my hair, not really in the mood to be judged.

He threw his hands up in surrender before going to the shelf of liquor and grabbing a shot glass. Placing it in front of me, he poured it to the rim and closed the bottle. Taking the glass, I took it to the head and slammed the glass on the counter before tilting my head back and hissing. Taking a deep breath, I asked for another shot. Taking it back again, I let the tears stain my face as the burning sensation took over my throat like a virus. *Don't Judge Me* by Chris Brown played softly through the speakers of the empty bar.

"You okay?" asked the bartender with a concerned look on his face.

"Yeah, I'm fine." I lied with a weak smile.

I was in the bar for hours drinking until my vision grew blurry. Running my fingers through my hair and taking a deep breath, I fished for my keys from my pocket and stumbled all the way to my car. As soon as I tried to open the car door, I felt someone close it back from behind me. Turning around, I was face to face with Jayceon who held a concerned look on his face.

"You okay?" he asked holding me up from almost hitting the ground.

"I'm fine." I slurred trying to get into my car again, but he closed it again.

"No, Come on, you're drunk. You're not getting in that car."

"I go wherever the fuck I wanna go, and don't be fucking touching me! Don't you have a wife to go to?" I slurred, pushing him off of me once more.

"Stop!" he yelled in my face, holding me by my shoulders.

I didn't know if it was just from me being intoxicated or my emotions being all over the place, but I burst into tears and slouched to the ground. He bended down to my level and grabbed my face pulling it close to his.

"Stop crying. Look, I'm gonna take you home."

"I wanna go home. Back to Houston." I cried, closing my eyes tight trying to blink away the tears that came pouring in after.

"Once you sober up you can go back home."

I nodded before he helped me off the ground and got me in my car. I gave him my keys and he drove off out of the parking lot. I didn't even know where he was taking me, and I was so intoxicated that I could barely see straight. Tilting my head back, I felt my eyes get heavy and before I knew it, I was out like a light.

"Cameron, come on babe, I'm tired." I groaned tilting my head back.

It was going on twelve in the morning and Cameron and I had been out damn near all day. I enjoyed the day we had together, but I had class in the morning, and I was beyond tired.

"Aight right after this stop we can go home."

"No, I want to go home now. I have class tomorrow and Jalisa's babysitter has been blowing me up since eight."

"I can pay her for staying over. I said I gotta make one more stop and we can go home."

"Fine." I groaned running my hands down my face in annoyance.

"Just go to sleep and I'll carry you in the house when we get there."

"You know I can't go to sleep in this car."

"I'm gonna need you to shut the fuck up! If I said wait until we get there that's what the fuck you gonna do!" he yelled slamming on breaks, making me jerk forward.

I kept my eyes forward, scared to look into his eyes. I already knew to just be quiet until we got to where we were heading. I wasn't in the mood, neither did I have the strength to physically fight him tonight. I pulled my phone from my bra and texted the babysitter warning her that I wasn't going to be home anytime soon. I kept my head in my phone at all cost trying to avoid him.

"Don't do that?"

"Do what, Cam?" I sighed looking out the window watching the rain trickled down the glass.

"Act like that."

"I don't feel like fighting with you tonight so I'm just gonna shut up."

"Aight, Mya." he replied dismissing me as if I were his child.

He pulled over to the nearby sidewalk, killing the engine. He took out a pair of black gloves and threw on his hoodie before getting out of the car. I didn't even question him because I knew he was going to put his hands on me. He'd nearly beat the daylights out of me one time, just for me asking him where he was during the day. I watched as he disappeared down an alley. I pulled my phone out scrolling through my call log, stopping by my mother's number. Swallowing the lump in my throat I clicked her name, finally getting over the fear and anxiety I'd been holding in for months. It had been a year since I'd run off with my sister and she hadn't thought to contact me, and it had been the other way around for me. I'd been working at the strip club for that time and met Cameron along the way. He was technically from Baton Rouge, but he was on business down there. He gave me that sanctuary I was in desperate need for; he gave me the comfort I'd never felt, even from my own mother. He was there for me when I needed him. There for me when I was all alone. He was the one who encouraged me daily to try and talk to my mother. Even though there was a bad side to him, all the good in him seemed to outshine the bad whenever his bad erupted from him like a volcano.

I pressed the phone to my ear and my heart dropped just from hearing my stepdad's voice.

"Hello?"

"Can I speak to my mom?" I asked not having the energy to fight with him either.

"She doesn't want to speak to you. She doesn't want you. You up and left her and had the nerve to take her other child with you. You're a sorry excuse for a fucking daughter and you have the nerve to call my wife phone with this bullshit?!"

"Will, give my mama the fucking phone!" I replied wiping my eyes.

"Hm, I don't think so. Don't call this damn phone again. If your number pop up one more time, I'm gonna show you how serious I can get. Don't come around my family nor get in touch with us."

"Will, I just want to talk to my mother and my brother." I cried.

"Goodbye, Samya." he replied clicking off.

I threw my phone on the floor and pulled my knees to my chest as I cried my eyes out. It was no secret that I missed my mother. Even though she was like a robot that was controlled by her damn husband, she was still my mother. I had memories of the old her. Memories of when it was just me, her, and my real father. The father that went missing years ago and was nowhere on this earth to be found.

I dried my face and my attention went to Cameron's phone, watching it blink multiple times. Curiosity filled my mind as I reached for his phone praying that he didn't come back and see me holding it in my hands. Putting the password in, I went to the messages and seen multiple numbers that weren't saved. Scanning the messages, my mind was racing a mile per minute. There were photos of naked women, who were beat up and bruised and strangers asking for prices. I jumped and screamed when the phone started to ring in my hand. Placing the phone back on the seat, I grabbed my purse and decided to get the hell out of dodge. I knew Cameron sold drugs, but I wasn't aware that he was deeper into shit. I literally was looking at a long list of women who were being auctioned.

Closing the door quietly, I looked around being unfamiliar with the area. Before I knew it, I began to run down the road with my heart beating faster than a track star. My heart nearly dropped out of my ass when I heard footsteps running behind me. I was almost close to a crowded area before I was snatched and dragged back, kicking and screaming. I was pulled into the alley where Cameron was standing in front of four women who were bound, lying on the ground with a few other guys beside him.

"This your girl?" asked the man dropping me to the ground.

"Where you going?" asked Cam walking up to me and squatting down to my level. I was so scared that I pissed myself and my lip began to tremble, scared of what he was going to do to me.

"I said where the fuck were you going?!" he yelled grabbing me roughly by my chin and slamming his fist into my face. I yelped in pain holding my face. My tears mixed with the rain that covered my face.

"I was leaving." I stuttered tasting the blood on my lip.

"So, you just was gonna up and leave me? After I put clothes on your back? After I gave you a place to fucking stay? After I put a roof over your hoe ass sister's head?"

"I'm sorry." I cried.

"Nah, I mean you always wanted to be in my business. I might as well show you what the fuck I do. Baby meet the bitches that put the clothes on your back." He said pulling his gun out and pointing at the girls on the ground who cries and screams were muffled.

"Let me go and I promise I won't say anything." I cried.

"Nah, see I think I be too lenient on you. I don't punish you how you need to be punished. See, you my girl and you always try to overstep your boundaries. So imma show you how I do these bitches on the streets. Yo Teddy," he replied nodding to the guy next to him.

The guy next to him grabbed one of the girls from the ground and untied her before ripping her clothes off. She started pleading and crying and even though I didn't understand her because she was speaking a different language, I knew she was begging for her life.

"Cam, stop, please!" I cried trying to break free from the man who was holding me back.

I watched as they took turns with her and even sodomized her with a metal pole. I watched as her blood mixed with the rain, running off. I was doing so much screaming and yelling that my voice grew hoarse. My eyes grew wide when he dragged the girl's half lifeless body towards me and placed her face near mine.

"Help me." she muttered half dead.

BANG!

I screamed to the top of my lungs as blood splattered all over my face.

"Wake up! It's just a dream!" yelled Jayceon, holding me tightly in his arms.

I was screaming to the top of my lungs drenched in sweat. I looked up at him feeling embarrassed. No one was ever there for me when I was having one of my nightmares and it felt weird having someone hold me and shake me back to reality. He stared into my eyes and pulled me closer into his chest rocking me; holding me like he felt my pain.

"Don't judge me." I sniffled.

"I would never judge you."

Chapter 9: Daddy's Home

Cameron

"Grey, you got a visitor?" said Officer Rodriguez, holding the cuffs in his hand.

"Who?"

"You'll see when you get there, come on."

"Stop acting hard, your coworkers on the other side. Now who the fuck here to see me? You know I don't like un-announced visitors."

"It's your mother."

"What she want?"

"I don't know, but she said it's important."

I shook my head before spreading my legs and holding my arms out for him to cuff me. Once he cuffed me, he escorted me through the gates and into the visitation area. I spotted my mother sitting at the table playing with her nails. As soon as she saw me her face lit up with glee.

"Hey mama," I smiled sitting down.

"Hey baby. How you been?" she asked placing my hands in hers.

"I'm living."

"Well, I know your birthday is in two days and I got the best gift for you."

"Mama you know I can't have certain shit in here."

"Son, this gift is something you're gonna love, trust me."

"Alright ma, what is it."

"Guess."

"I don't have time to guess. You know these visits are timed."

"You coming home!"

"Ma, I done hired damn near every good lawyer I could find. I damn near went broke getting one that could shorten my time. It's time for you to accept it, I'm in here for eighty plus."

"Can you shut up, boy, and listen. I went to New York and I've been working with some private investigators and got a new lawyer. Baby, you get out on your birthday!"

"What?" I asked with a smile as big as the sea.

"You heard me, son, you getting out in two days!"

"Nobody told me anything."

"Because I asked them to let me tell you. Son, I can't wait till get you home!" she smiled, wiping the tears of joy from her eyes. I stood up and she embraced me in her arms.

"No touching!" said the guard, making me look at him as if he'd lost his mind.

He cleared his throat before turning his head. It was no secret that I had connection on the inside. Everybody in that bitch knew not to give me any trouble or I was going to cause trouble, and whenever I caused trouble, I wreaked havoc. My mother sat back down and smiled even harder.

"I know you happy that I'm coming home, but you smiling a little too hard."

"I gotta tell you something else."

"More good news?"

"Yes, news you've been wanting for a long time."

"Talk to me, ma."

"Guess who I saw?"

"Who?"

"Just guess."

"Ma you know I don't like this guessing game."

"I saw Samya."

Just from the sound of her name being said, a smile spread across my face. Just knowing that she was in the same state as me, made me feel some type of way. A wave of excitement rushed through my body like electricity. I was happy and just from my mother telling me that she saw her, made me eager to walk out of prison and go see her that very moment. To go apologize for the crazy shit I put her through, to hold her and most importantly hold my son.

"Did she have my son with her?"

"Sadly no. She was really trying to avoid me. I'm far from stupid, I think that girl is hiding something. I've been in this town for years and I've searched high and low for Samya, and all of sudden she pops right up out of the blue. I love that girl as my daughter in-law but something's off."

"Ain't nothing off. If you see her and she still in town, do me a favor."

"What favor."

"Go into my account and take out five thousand. After you do that, go pick out something nice for her and tell her it's from me; add the money to it too. Drop it off to her grandmother's spot."

"Son, I don't think that's a good approach fo-."

"I said drop it off! I'm not having this conversation with you right now, ma."

"You gonna watch how the fuck you talk to me, Cameron. I'm your mother, you're not my damn father! As I was fucking saying, I don't think that's a good approach right now. She hasn't seen you in six years, Cameron."

"If you don't do it, I'll get somebody else to do it."

"Okay, I'll do it, Cameron."

"Nah, it's fine. I'll get Teddy to do it."

"I got her number if you want me to give it to you."

"You already know I want her number."

"Okay, I'll write it down for you."

"How did you get her number?"

"From her stepfather." she replied writing it down on a slip of paper and sliding it towards me.

"Time's up!" said the guard stepping in.

I gave my mother a smile before being escorted to the back, feeling completely different. Feeling like a different man I was before I walked out of my cell a few minutes prior. Once I was escorted back to my cell, Rodriguez uncuffed me.

"What you looking happy for?" he asked with a raised brow, leaning against the bars.

"I gotta make a call."

"You know I can't let you do that. We still on lockdown and I risked my job just letting you out for a visit."

"Save that bullshit excuse for the birds. Give me your phone."

He sighed shaking his head with a hesitating look. "You got five minutes." he replied giving me his phone as he kept watching.

I pulled the piece of paper from my jumpsuit and dialed the number. A smile wider than the Cheshire cat spread across my face when I heard her voice.

"Hello?" her voice rung through the phone.

I was so strung from hearing her voice that I didn't even notice that she'd hung up. Just from hearing how much more developed her voice was, how differently she sounded made me intrigued on what else changed. Dialing the number again she answered once more, this time more annoyed.

"Who is this?

"You know exactly who this is."

The line went so quiet, I could hear how heavy she was breathing.

"Daddy's coming home."

<h1 style="text-align:center">Samya</h1>

Hanging up my phone, I blocked the number and turned my phone completely off. As bad as I wanted to have an anxiety attack, I was shocked that I kept my composure.

"You okay?" asked Jayceon, getting back into the car with bags of food.

"Yeah, I'm fine." I smiled taking my bag from him.

"You sure."

"Yes, I'm fine."

"Alright, just making sure."

"Thank you."

"It's nothing. I gotta stop by my center real fast and then I can drop you off home."

"That's fine."

He nodded before cranking the car up and pulling out of the parking lot. I turned my attention to him, just staring at his features. The way his tattoos cascaded down his arms like a river. The way his muscles relaxed when he was focused.

"I wanna apologize."

"For what?" he asked with a raised brow.

"For being a burden. You've literally been here for me multiple times whenever I'm in need of someone."

"I wasn't going to sit there and let you go through all of that by yourself."

"I'm *technically* a stranger, why?"

"I don't care who you are. I'm a mentor, I guess it was just an instinct to be that shoulder to cry on."

"Mentor?"

"Yeah, I mentor kids and everything."

"I wish you could mentor my deviant lil brother."

"Probably could."

"Trust me, the only person that boy listens to is my Nana. Him and I got into it that day you picked me up from the bar."

"Who is he?"

"Seven."

"Tall light skin dude? Hazel's son?"

"Yeah." I replied, tucking my lips and sighing just from hearing my mother's name.

"I mentor him already."

"No offense but he's still doing crazy shit."

"There's not much I can do with him. But whenever he's going through it, I'm the first person he comes to."

"Got any tips for him to give me respect?"

"Seven is gonna do him regardless. He's not gonna respect you unless he knows that you understand him."

"If you say so." I scoffed, popping a fry in my mouth.

"But I got a question for you."

"Wassup?"

"Why you so stuck up? Not asking to be rude." he laughed.

"I'm not stuck up."

"Yeah right."

"Mhm, okay since we asking questions. Does your wifey pooh know you're out with another girl?" I asked wiggling my eyebrows making him laugh.

"She'll be aight, I mean it's not like I'm doing anything out of the ordinary with you. I'm a faithful ass man. Trust me, I love that girl." he smiled thinking of her.

"Aw that's cute." I smiled shrugging my shoulders against his.

"Stop." he laughed.

"No, for real. I always get happy when I see powerful cute ass couples."

"Yeah right. What about you?"

"What about me?"

"You got anybody special back in Houston?"

"Nope, nobody."

"Why you say it like that?"

"Because I'm not looking for anybody. All my life I've been trying to get myself together. Build myself up to become this person who I've always dreamed of being. Successful, smart, and a provider."

"How's that coming along?"

"Pretty good so far. I raised my little sister as if she were my daughter. I think I did amazing with her." I smiled just thinking about how good I'd done with raising Jalisa.

"Got any kids?"

"No." I replied looking down at my hands.

"Want any?"

"Of course. I always wanted twins; A boy and a girl to be exact."

"Twins? I don't know about all that."

"I bet if your girl had twins you would know about it then. Twins aren't that bad." I laughed.

"Yeah right. I pray for whatever nigga you get with."

"Shut up."

He pulled into the parking lot of his community center and parked up front. Killing the engine, he took his seatbelt off and got out. Catching me off guard, he came to my side and opened the door, helping me out of the car.

"I never said I was going to come in."

"Well, I want you to."

"I look like somebody's mama right now." I laughed looking down at my Adidas sweatpants, white T, and slides with different colored socks.

"You look good, now come on." he laughed walking through the double doors.

As soon as we went inside, my jaw dropped in awe looking around. There were flyer's promoting neighborhood activities, expensive furniture, and a map on the wall that showed the entire building. I looked in amazement as I walked down the hall that had exquisite paintings aligning the wall.

"This is beautiful." I smiled stopping in my tracks, staring at the painting of a mother holding a child in her arms with roses blooming around it.

"Oh yeah, I have a few kids who come here and paint. This was done by Mariah. She was adopted at a young age and her foster family only got her for the check. So, she comes here to get a piece of mind."

"Well she did an amazing job. I wish I could buy this."

"I can ask her for you. I mean she does sell most of her paintings. Some paintings she only does for display here."

"Oh okay."

We walked up to the front desk and Jayceon was met with an older woman. She pulled him into a hug and kissed his forehead before bringing her attention to me.

"Hey Samya, this is my mother Jerolyn. Mama this is Samya."

"Please tell me this ya new girlfriend because that wife of yours," she laughed.

"Ma stop, this is Ms. Gale's granddaughter."

"I ain't know Gale had another grandchild. Baby who yo mama?" she asked.

"Hazel." I smiled weakly.

"I ain't know Hazel had another child. I thought it was just Seven and Jamir."

"No ma'am it's me and my other sister."

"Oh okay, well nice to meet you, hun." she smiled bringing me into a hug.

"Nice to meet you too."

"Alright, now I'll see y'all later. I gotta go start this yoga class, I've had them kids in there waiting for me for a good fifteen minutes."

I nodded and waved goodbye watching her disappear into another room. I looked over at Jayceon with a proud look.

"Wow, this place is amazing."

"Thank you, I try." he laughed.

"No seriously, this is amazing. You did a great job here."

"Thanks again. But you can sit in here for a few, I gotta go to my office and get some stuff."

I nodded watching him go down the hall and walk into a room. Sitting down in the waiting area, I pulled my phone from my pocket and turned it back on, praying that Cameron didn't try to contact me again. Shooting Una a text, my mind wandered to me only being here for three more days; wandering to the thought of me having to go back to my life in Houston. I looked up when the sound of heels clicking on the tile floors alerted my ears. The woman took off her shades and looked around.

"Hey who are you looking for?" I asked hoping that I could be any assistance. She looked over at me in utter disgust. Keeping my composure, I gave her the same dirty look she gave me.

"Yes, I'm looking for my husband, Jayceon. The man who owns this place." she replied with an attitude.

"He's in his office."

"Mm, okay." she replied walking past me flipping her hair.

"Boujie bitch." I mumbled and rolled my eyes.

"What you doin here?" asked Seven, coming from out of what looked like a gym. He was drenched in sweat holding a basketball.

"I'm here minding my business. I thought you were gonna walk past me and not say shit like we been doing."

"Well, I need a ride home anyway."

"I didn't drive."

"Well pay for me an Uber."

"You really asking me to pay for you an Uber the way you talked to me."

"I'll fucking walk."

"No, you're not, I told you I was coming to get you." said Will coming towards us.

We locked eyes on each other, and I stood up ready to unleash all my anger out on him. I was ready to beat the dog shit out of him and I didn't give a fuck if he had Cancer. This nigga could be on his last leg and I would still beat the breaks off him.

"Samya?" he asked trying to figure out if it was really me.

I felt as if all my words were caught in the back of my throat and I couldn't find the first thing I wanted to say. Finally, just deciding to keep my mouth shut, I grabbed my purse and walked out the door heading back to the car.

Chapter 10: The New Me

Jayceon

"Who the fuck is that girl, Jay?" asked Sabrina sitting on my desk with her arms crossed.

"You really gonna bust up in my office like that. I don't get a hey or how you doing or nothing?"

"Don't play with me, Jay."

"I have a lot of females that come in here and my mother works with them. Don't come in here starting your shit."

"Starting my shit?"

"Yes."

"Answer my question."

"I don't ever question you about the off the wall shit you and your friends do. Why do you question me about irrelevant shit? Every time a girl is in the same building as me you go off. Have the same faith I have in you, and don't be stressing my baby out over dumb shit either."

"Whatever, Jay." she replied huffing like a toddler.

"You must be horny, tired, or hungry to be coming in here acting up like this."

"I'm all three." she replied, throwing her head back.

"Well I can't do nothing right now, wait until I get home."

"Boy if you don't bend me over and fuck me over this desk!" she replied pushing stuff off my desk and trying to hike up her dress. I rushed over to her and stopped her, ignoring her groan.

"The lock on my door still ain't fixed yet, and remember my mama walked in on us last time. I don't have time for that this time."

"Push something up to the door."

"Look, go home and I'll follow you there after I finish handling business. I got you, baby." I smiled pulling her closer to me and pecking her lips.

"Hurry up!" She smiled against my lips, gripping my dick through my sweats.

"I will, now get ready for daddy." I smiled.

She straightened out her clothes before walking out the doors. After grabbing my folder filled with important dates and meetings, I made my way out. Scanning the area, I didn't see Samya in sight. Going outside, a wave of relief rained over me when I saw her in my car. Getting inside, I noticed the displeased look on her face.

"You good?" I asked.

"I'm Gucci."

"Aight, well I can take you home now."

"Thanks.

Cranking my Range up, I pulled out the parking lot and made my way to her house. After dropping her off, I made my way straight home. In the midst of listening to my music, it was cut off by my ringing phone. I groaned seeing Ace's name flash on the screen. This nigga held a conversation like it was a business meeting. He talked more than a bitch half the time. Sliding my finger across the screen I heard him and Jace going back and forth.

"Nigga, I said imma tell him." Said Jace.

"He already on the phone now, nigga."

"If y'all gonna argue like a couple of bitches y'all can call me back." I sighed.

"Yo, we know you busy and all but our boy George in town." Said Jace.

"George from college?"

"Yeah nigga! We out at the bar right now. You down?"

"Nah, I promised Sabrina I would come home."

"Nigga if you don't take off them heels and take that tampon out yo ass. Sabrina ugly ass will be aight."

"What I tell you about talking about my wife."

"Yo wife know I don't like her bean head ass."

"Look man, we can meet up tomorrow. George don't head back to New York until next week." Said Jace.

"Say word. I'm down."

"Yeah, ya boy getting married."

"George hoe ass finally settling down?" I asked laughing, not believing my ears.

"Yeah man, they been together for three years."

"If wifing a bitch gone turn me into a bitch, I don't want it." Said Ace jokey ass.

"Don't nobody want yo dumb ass." Said Jace.

"Nigga you dumb." Ace retaliated.

"Aight well hit me back later, I gotta go." I said while pulling into my yard.

A smirk spread across my face seeing Sabrina's Rolls Royce Parked in my spot. I hung up the phone and went inside, smelling the aroma of cinnamon lit up the air. Making my way upstairs, I walked past Micah's room door. Closing the door, I went across the hall to where my bedroom was located. Opening the door, a flirtatious smirk formed on my face once again when I saw Sabrina butt ass naked on top of the white silk sheets.

"I've been waiting for you." She smiled gripping one of her breasts, biting down on her lip. I pulled my shirt from over my head and kicked the door closed before approaching her and picking her up. Wrapping her legs around my waist, I gently laid her down on the bed, parting her legs ready to give her what she'd been begging for.

Seven

"You didn't tell me your sister was in town." said my dad pulling into the yard.

"Because it's irrelevant."

"That's how you feel?"

"You know that's how I feel."

"Would have thought you would have had a change in mind. You always wanted her to come back home and now she's here."

"Yeah here for the wrong fucking reason." I scoffed.

"Still mad at her?"

"Yeah, I'm fucking livid! She come here with the wrong fucking intentions. She's only here to try and prove a fucking point. She not here for me, she was never here to come and get me!"

"Son, Samya is gonna continue to be the selfish bitch she is. She's always been that way."

"I know, you told me."

"So, you gonna tell your mama?"

"That's none of my concern. Mama don't wanna see her ass."

"I don't know, maybe you could talk to her about it."

"I will later." I replied pulling a cigarette from my pack and lighting it.

"You know my lungs can't take that shit, get out my car."

"My bad, I forgot pops." I replied putting it out and getting out of the car.

"When's your next chemo appointment?"

"Next week."

"Aight, I'll be there."

He nodded before walking into the house leaving me on the porch. Sitting down, I re-lit my cigarette and watched the ongoing cars pass by. It was starting to get dark and for some reason, I found the enjoyment of the night wind rippling up against my skin. Feeling my phone ring in my pocket, I pulled it out seeing Jalisa's name flash across the screen. Sliding my finger across the screen, I answered her Facetime call and her face lit up with joy.

"Hey." she smiled.

"Wassup."

"I thought you were supposed to call me last night."

"I got busy." I shrugged.

"I got good news."

"What it is?"

"I got the scholarship I've been working so hard to get. I literally have a full paid ride to go to Spelman, my dream school! You don't know how hard I've worked." she smiled doing a happy dance.

"That's cool." I replied taking another pull from my cigarette.

"That's it?" she asked with a raised brow.

"What more do you want me to say?"

"An *oh I'm so happy for you. lil sis*, would mean a lot you know?"

"You should already know I am; I shouldn't have to say it."

"I can't believe you right now, Sev." she scoffed shaking her head.

"Look. I had a long day, lil sis. Hit me back in the morning."

"You know what, screw it. I know you and Mya aren't on the best foot, but you don't have to shut me out like a stranger. This is why I don't call you."

"Lisa, wait."

She hung up the phone and I sighed before running one hand down my face. The last thing I wanted to do was upset her when she didn't do anything to me.

"What you lookin like a stressed-out baby daddy for?" said Mariah walking up on me with her hands in her pocket.

"Psh, you don't know the half of it."

"Trust me, I'm going through it worse than you." she laughed lightly, sitting next to me.

"I doubt it."

"Aight, you go first." she replied, taking my cigarette and taking a pull from it.

"My pops got lung cancer, my Nana got cancer, my job search is going shitty because of my record, I got a feeling my mama back on that shit, I owe money to people, my lil sister pissed off at me, and my big sister who's sitting on cash is down here acting like shit gucci when it's not."

"Damn babe," she sighed, shaking her head.

"Your go."

"My foster parents got three more kids, adding to the four others living in our three-bedroom section eight apartment. The little bit of money I make from working at the dry cleaners go towards the kids. My foster dad has been giving me these looks like I won't blow his fucking brains out, so I have to sleep with one eye open, and I met up with my biological mother yesterday and she threatened to shoot me if I didn't get off her property. That bitch gave me up when I was three years old and look at her now, living it up with three other kids."

"Damn, Ryah." I sighed, pulling her into a hug.

"It's fine, I'm living."

"Nah, I mean Ryah, you nineteen. You have permission to leave whenever you want to."

"Then where am I going to go, Sev?"

"I don't know, but you need to get the fuck up out of there. Regardless, once you turn twenty-one you're not allowed to be there anymore."

"I know this, but I plan on leaving once I get my shit together."

"Hopefully that's soon."

"It is." she replied throwing the cigarette butt in the grass.

"Yo Mariah, bring yo ass on!" said her foster brother, Trell, walking over and snatching her up. I stood up and grabbed her back, looking at dude as if he was fucking crazy. He wasn't going to put his hands on her like that in front of me.

"Get yo fucking hands off her! One thing you won't do is jack her up like that in front of me."

"Nigga I'll blow yo fucking brains out on the pavement right now without doing the fucking time. This my got damn sister!" he replied pulling her back.

"Trell, let me go! I said I was coming home."

"Well I don't know how the fuck you're gonna get there. You got Fatima blowing my damn phone up asking me to pick yo ass up." he replied referring to their foster mother.

"I'll get her home."

"Nah nigga, she good. I got it."

"Trell, I'm fucking fine. Go home!"

They stared each other down for a good minute or two before he scoffed and got in his car, speeding off down the pavement.

"Let's start walking, it's a thirty-minute walk to your apartment anyway."

"I'm sorry about that."

"I'm not worried about that nigga."

"I see that." She replied, getting up from the porch.

"So, tell me about this evil sister of yours." She laughed.

"I'm not even about to get on that conversation. Let's talk about this art you putting out."

"What about it?"

"You making big bucks off of it."

"I know. Jayceon hit me up and told me someone was interested in buying my artwork."

"That's dope, you talented though."

"Yeah, I know but I feel like I'm wasting my talent staying here. Like you said, I can leave anytime. The only thing that's keeping me here really, is my actual baby brother. I know if I leave, I can't take him with me."

"In order to get custody of him you have to have a stable environment for yourself. If you try and do that here, I doubt you'll get anywhere."

"Okay, where should I go then."

"Anywhere but here." I laughed.

"Your smile is everything, I'm telling you dude. I wanna take a picture and paint you."

"You better go somewhere with that Van Goat shit."

"First of all, his name is Van Gogh. Who is the goat nigga?"

she laughed, shoving me.

"I guess."

"But for real though, you too cute to be walking around here mean mugging and shit like you do."

"Cute is for animals."

"Okay, you too fucking fine to be walking around here like somebody done stole your fucking puppy."

"You think I'm fine?" I laughed, stopping in my tracks and popping my collar.

"This is why I don't tell you shit; you always get a big head."

"I love getting compliments from you. At least I know you be telling the truth. You the only person in my life right now who ain't scared to keep it real with me."

"Same with you. I know you're always gonna keep it real with me too." she smiled pulling me into a hug.

I moved one of her curls from her face and smiled down at her. Before she could say anything, a black Range Rover pulled up on us. Out of instinct, I pushed Mariah behind me and reached for my gun in my pants.

"Hold up partner, it ain't that kind of party." said Teddy rolling his window down.

"Don't be rolling up on me like that. What you want, Ted?" I asked, not really in the mood for his bullshit.

"You know what I'm here for."

"I said I would have your money by next week."

"You said that shit last week, Seven." he replied getting out of the car with a bunch of other dudes.

"It takes all that for poor lil ol me." I laughed shaking my head.

"Laughing in my face is like playing with your life." he replied pulling his gun from his waist and putting it to my head, but I was so quick that I had mine already pressed up to his face. I had five guns drawn on me. Any other moment I wasn't afraid to die but since I had Mariah with me, I was scared shitless.

"You always were quick with that gun, but you can't take all of us out with five bullets."

"I said I'll get your money."

"Take that gun out my face before I give them the okay to light you and your bitch up."

Hesitant at first, I swallowed the huge lump in my throat before looking back at Mariah, who was in full blown tears. Lowering my gun, they snatched it from my hand. Teddy was far from a small dude and the way he jacked me up against the car damn near took the life out of me.

"See, boss man was always generous when it came to you because technically your family. But one thing we won't do is disrespect and lies. Now either you pay me now, or I'll take your life and that'll pay your debt. Three thousand ain't a small sum of cash."

"I gave you a thousand two days ago!" I felt my body go numb when he punched me so hard in my mouth, I heard my jaw crack.

"Leave him alone." cried Mariah trying to break free of the grip one of the guys had on her.

"That down payment was taken as a late fee, you still owe us three."

"I don't have it."

"You don't have it?" he asked with a chuckle.

"You heard me."

He dropped me to the ground and next thing I knew they were going blow for blow on me. I laid on the ground in a fatal position trying to cover my face. All I could hear was Mariah's cries for them to let me go. Her cries were then growing faint.

Chapter 11: A Little More Love

Seven

"Stop it! I'll give you your money! Just let him go!" yelled Mariah.

They stopped in the act when they heard her mention money. I looked up with a half, blurred vision seeing Mariah dig in her pocket and pull out cash.

"Here, this is nine hundred so far and I'll pay the rest tomorrow, I promise." she said shoving the cash at Teddy.

"This fucking chump change." he scoffed, counting it.

"I said I'll have the rest tomorrow; I promise! Just please leave him alone!"

Teddy walked up to her and snatched her wallet from her. Taking her license out, he snapped a picture of it.

"Mariah Tahari Jackson, 1957 North Ardenwood, age nineteen, Born July 24. Oh, you a Gemini? Just for you being a Gemini, I'll give you until tomorrow night. If I don't have my money, I'll air Ardenwood Village the fuck out! You hear me?" he said getting in her face.

"I hear you."

"Good."

He signaled for his boys to get back in the car before driving off. Mariah knelt down to my level and pulled me into her lap with tears cascading down her cheeks.

"What the fuck, Seven?!" she yelled, rocking me in her arms.

"I'm sorry." I replied coughing up blood.

"No, come on, we're not gonna make it to my place. Too many people are over there, we have to turn back."

"Okay."

"Once we get to your house, we have to take you to the hospital."

"I can't go, I don't have insurance. I've taken worse ass whippings than this, I'll be fine." I replied limping towards my house.

"I can't believe your ass right now! If you didn't have the money to pay them back, you could have asked me."

"You know I don't like asking for money."

"I don't give a fuck what you don't like, Seven. They almost fucking killed you in front of me!"

"But they didn't."

"If I didn't have such a good fucking heart, I would leave your ass here and let you limp your ass all the way fucking home." she replied trying her best to keep calm.

"I'm sorry, Ryah. I should have never put you in that situation and I promise you I will pay you back."

"Nigga you couldn't even fucking give them the money, how the fuck you gonna pay me back?! I'm fucking ecstatic man!"

"I said I'm sorry."

"Whatever Seven." she replied helping me up the porch. We snuck up quietly to my room, trying not to cause attention to my mother who was sleeping on the couch. Opening my door, Mariah helped me get on the bed before closing it shut.

"Do you mind if I sleep over here tonight? I'll deal with my foster parents tomorrow."

"Yeah, you can stay."

Walking over to my mirror, I winced in pain when I raised my arms to take my shirt off. Looking in the mirror, Mariah walked over and traced her finger along the bruises on my chest and side.

"You okay?" she asked, massaging the area gently.

"Yeah, I'm fine. Growing up here I always got my ass beat worse than this. It barely hurt."

"Can you stop trying to be a fucking bad ass for just a moment. Seven your human like everybody else. If I got my ass whipped the way you did, I would probably be crying right now."

"Well you didn't." I replied pulling my sweats off, leaving me in nothing but my boxers.

"Look, I'm gonna go and get something to clean your face up with."

I nodded before sitting down on the end of my bed and watching her walk across the hall to the bathroom. Within minutes she came back with a hot rag in her hand. She knelt down in front of me and began to clean the blood off of my face.

"Why did you stay? Why did you offer to pay them? And where are you getting three thousand dollars from?"

"Seven, don't start."

"No seriously. Ever since I met you last year at the center all you ever do is help me. Even when you didn't know me you helped me. Why are you still here for me whenever I push you away?"

"Because I used to be you. Every time someone tried to be there for me and care for me, I pushed them away. You know what happens whenever I push them away? They disappear and I never see them again. Then it's too late to want to receive that care and love from someone because they're no longer there."

"Damn."

"Yeah, damn indeed. When I love, I love hard and I'll do anything to protect the person I care about."

"You love me?"

"I've always loved you." she replied, putting down the rag and sitting next to me.

I was so used to not receiving love and affection in my own home, that it felt unreal to have somebody I actually cared about show me that love and affection. She grabbed me by my face and pressed her lips to mine. Pulling back, I grabbed her chin and pecked her lips once more.

"I love you too."

"If you love me stop slinging drugs."

"Ryah you know that's my only income right now. It's fast money." I replied, laying back looking at the ceiling.

"Your only income nearly got both of us killed. Your only income has put your ass in jail multiple times. Seven, just how do you know if next time you won't get lucky?"

"If I stop then what can I do?"

"I know the manager at Walmart, I can get you there."

"I ain't bagging no fucking grocery." I scoffed.

"Yes, the fuck you are! So be prepared to fill out these applications for tomorrow."

"Aight, I'll stop." I gave in once I saw the serious look on her face.

"Promise me."

"I promise."

"Good." she replied lying right beside me.

Jalisa

"Yo come on, it'll be fun." begged my friend Rena.

"I don't know."

"Come on, please! Look, it's an eleven-hour drive. Your sister doesn't come back until Monday. You got three days. We'll be down there for two days and come back that Sunday night."

"I'll think about it."

"You don't have time to think about it. Look, it'll give us an opportunity to tour the college by ourselves, party, and they also got a Morehouse game Saturday night."

"You know what, fuck it, I'm in." I replied getting out of bed and closing my laptop.

"Alright, get ready cause I know I'm ready." she replied jumping up and down in excitement.

"But wait, what about money? I've never been to Atlanta and I know certain shit is expensive. And Lord knows I don't want to be stuck at a busted Motel 6 with roaches."

"My aunt lives there; we can stay with her."

"Did you ask though."

"She ain't seen me in a good minute, I'm pretty sure she'll enjoy my company." she laughed.

"Yeah whatever. Go warm the car up so we can go. The sooner, the better."

"I knew you would give in. We've been talking about this all week."

"Yeah but one condition."

"What?"

"I'm inviting Kevin."

"No, this is a girl thing."

"Come on! Kevin is from Atlanta; he can show us around."

"You barely know the dude. I mean yeah he helped you out at the party but still, you don't know homeboy."

"Still, I just don't wanna go down there half blind."

"You're not. Now while you pack your mini suitcase, I'm gonna use your car to go to my house and pack."

"Alright, don't wreck my shit." I replied throwing my keys at her.

"I won't. Kisses."

I watched her walk out the door and as soon as I heard my car pull out the yard, I stood up and went to my closet preparing myself to pack. After packing two days of clothes, I sat at the end of my bed waiting on Rena to bring my car back. Staring off into space my mind quickly wandered to how unsupportive Seven was when I told him the news. Jamir and Samya congratulated me and couldn't shut up about it. It was him on the other hand, who seemed like he didn't give a fuck. Even though I barely knew him growing up, I was trying to be that perfect little sister. As badly as I wanted to go to a school in Louisiana to be closer to the family I barely knew, I went with following my dreams. A part of me felt horrible for choosing that, when I'd talked down on Samya for choosing her dreams other than family.

I was knocked out of my deep thoughts by the front door being open. Raising a brow, I walked out of my room and looked over the stairwell to see nobody there.

"Rena?" I called walking further down, I received no answer.

"Rena if you're playing with me, I swear I'm calling this lil trip off."

"And where the hell are you going?" said Renny. sneaking up from a corner making me jump.

"Uh."

"Uh my ass. Where you and lil miss sneaky ass think y'all going."

"Aight bitch, I hope you packed because I'm ready to hit the ro-." said Rena bursting through the doors but she stopped mid-sentence once she saw Renny.

"What are you doing here, Renny?" I asked trying to change the subject.

"Trying to figure out where the hell the both of you think y'all going. Do I need to call Mya?"

"Please don't do that."

"Then tell me where we packed up and heading to."

"We're going to Atlanta for two days to tour Spelman." I muttered, putting my head down.

One thing I didn't like to do was disappoint people close to me. Renny was basically like an uncle to me. Samya and I lived with him for nearly three years and even though he was gay, he was technically the only father figure I'd had. He taught me things that Samya didn't have time to teach me because she was always working.

"What I tell you about looking down." he said lifting my chin up.

"I know."

"Okay then, I don't care how disappointed I may be in you, your eyes better remain up."

"I'm sorry."

"Don't blame her, I pushed her to come with me."

"Does Nancy know you sneaking away?" he asked, referring to her mother.

"No."

"Look, since it has to do with college, I'll keep it on the low. You know if Samya knew she would be on your ass like gravy on rice. You know she doesn't like you traveling far."

"I'll call you when I get there and before I go to bed, and I'll text you whenever I leave to come back home."

"You better," he sighed bringing me into a hug.

"I love you." I smiled, rocking him side to side.

"I love you too. But if Mya comes home early, I don't know what to tell you."

"I got that handled."

"Okay, well, be safe on your trip okay?"

I nodded before going back upstairs to grab my suitcase. Renny helped us put everything in the back of my car. After giving him a hug, I jumped in the driver's seat and Rena got in the passenger seat with a smile of excitement. When I noticed Renny at my window, I rolled it down.

"Be safe please."

"I will." I smiled.

"Good, now go before I change my mind."

He kissed my cheek before I rolled my window up and sped off down the road. After setting up my GPS, I prepared myself for an exhausting ride.

"Girl my lil friend just texted me." said Rena flashing her phone.

"Okay and?"

"And they got this huge party going on tomorrow night and we just got invited."

"I'm not going down there to party."

"Come on, one party won't hurt."

"The last party I went to, I ended up almost in jail."

"But you won't be in jail this time. You don't know anyone down there."

"I don't care, still."

"Okay, well you have a good bit of time to change your mind."

"I doubt I'll change my mind."

"I have faith in you." she smiled.

Chapter 12: Facing Demons

Samya

"When the hell did we start going to church on Fridays?" I asked Una, straightening out my dress.

"Nana had some huge announcement that she has to make in front of the church. You know everybody loves her and they'll come to church whenever she asks them to."

"Well, I'm going to need Nana to not make last minute plans like she just did."

"Well today is her birthday; you know we have to do whatever she asks today and not complain about it."

"I guess." I huffed.

"Come on girls." said my Nana coming into the room with her violet dress and matching hat on.

"Nana, you look good." I smiled walking over and bringing her into a hug.

"I always look good. I don't even look seventy-two today."

"You really don't." laughed Una, walking circles around her.

I inspected my grandmother's skin and even though the cancer was kicking her ass, she barely looked it. I would have to get up in the middle of the night and rush to her room because she would wake up coughing in a frenzy. Ever since I'd arrived here every night, I found myself moving from my room to hers. I found comfort sleeping in the same room as her, just to make sure she was okay.

One night I found myself staring at her while she was sleeping and just lying there silently crying. I didn't know when God was going to take her, and we always heard the same things when it came to doctor's visits. She wasn't improving and if she left me, I couldn't find it in myself to prepare myself mentally for it. I was already improving slightly day by day, recovering from the fucked-up childhood I'd had.

"Let's go before y'all be walking." she coughed, making Una and I pat her back in concern.

"You okay?" asked Una.

"I'm fine." she coughed.

"No, you're not."

"Yes, I am, stop worrying about me now."

"You've got chronic Leukemia and it's getting worse. How are you going to tell me to stop worrying?" I replied concerned.

"Let's go before we be late." she said walking out of the room.

"I can't believe her." I scoffed, running my hands through my hair.

"Just let it be. She still has hope, so I think it's best if we do too."

Una brought me into a hug before we gathered our things and met my Nana outside in her red Cadillac. The entire drive to the church, we joked around and listened to old school music. If I closed my eyes, I could imagine when Una and I were young, doing the same thing we were doing. We would sit in the back seat and sing along to the Temptations while my grandmother would ask us what we knew about that type of music. The nostalgia hit me like a brick once again. We pulled up to the church and damn near everybody and their mama were out there.

My grandmother pulled next to Jamir's car and killed the engine. Una and I got out before helping her inside.

"I don't need no help." she huffed, trying to push Una and I off her.

"Nana you left your cane at home, I don't want you to be walking around and be done fell over." I replied trying to hold onto her.

She didn't even argue back like I knew she wanted to because she knew I was right. She barely had any strength left in her and it was evident. After walking her up the stairs, we went inside and found a seat near Jamir, his wife, and his three kids. We sat through an hour of preaching before my Nana got up and went to the front receiving multiple applause.

"Good morning, church." she said through the mic receiving multiple replies.

"Most of you have known me to come here for years now. As we all know today, I'm getting older. Much older and my condition has worsened. I've found out today that I'm in my last stages of cancer but I don't want anyone to be discouraged and I wanted everyone to come here today so I could have time to be with the ones I love before God calls me home."

Looking around, the church was filled with family, family friends and a few people my grandmother helped around the community. The crowd returned various reactions and questions about her health and how she was feeling, were scattered all throughout the church. I didn't even notice I was crying until Jamir pulled me into a side hug. I spent thousands of dollars for chemo and surgeries and prayed damn near every night for her to improve, for her to stand in front of everyone and drop the bomb on us like that. It was uncalled for. I wasn't prepared to bury my grandmother and she knew if she would have told me privately, I would have caused a scene.

"I have to go to the bathroom." I told Jamir while standing up and walking out.

Making my way to the bathroom, I opened the doors and walked into the stall, closing it. Rolling some tissue off, I wiped my eyes trying to calm myself. For some reason, I pulled my phone out and went to my contacts. Staring at Jayceon's name, I sighed before powering my phone off. I needed that sense of comfort he was so willingly to provide. Whenever he told me everything was going to be okay, I believed him. I found that sense of sobriety that brought me back.

After recollecting myself, I opened the bathroom door. As soon as I stepped out, I stared face to face with the woman who caused me to be the way I was. The woman who I was so scared to talk to and confront. She looked at me in utter shock like she couldn't believe I was really standing here in front of her. I didn't know who was going to speak first but I knew for sure it wasn't going to be me. We stared each other down for a good five minutes before she finally took a deep breath, breaking the silence. She walked around me and went into the stall I was in. I didn't know if I was hallucinating or if she'd really walked past me and ignored me like I was a stranger on the streets.

"So, this is what we doing now?" I asked, leaning on the wall.

The fact that she sat in the stall and still said nothing to me made me want to fuck her up. The only thing that was stopping me from kicking the stall door down, was that I was in the church and it was a special day for my grandmother. Deciding to deal with her another time, I walked out the door and just my luck, I ended up bumping into Will. My eye instantly went to the little boy in his arms.

"Would have thought you would have missed something this big. You know this is a family matter?" he said, making me clench my fist.

The Lord was really testing me, and I had to fight the temptations to not put my hands on him. How could he be on the verge of dying and still walk around being this huge asshole?

"I'm gonna go before you get me out of character. Because once I lose myself and you see the other person in me, it's not worth it. I'm not going to let you intervene on the reason I'm here."

"Oh, now you so holy and sanctified. You act like your mama and I don't know what you been doing to get where you are now."

"As I said earlier, I'm gonna go before I bust a cap in your ass."

"Daddy, she said a bad word."

I raised my brow in curiosity. Did Will cheat on my mom and have a baby on her? There was no way this little boy was my brother. It couldn't be, and I knew it wasn't. My mom came out the bathroom and he began to reach for her. I was so in shock that I didn't know what to say or do.

"Lucas, say bye to your sister." said Will.

Jalisa

"Girl stop before your aunt hear us." I told Rena, watching her twerk and yell in her new outfit for the night.

"She knocked out off of Nyquil, you know she sick. My aunt Gina is out like a light."

"I know but still, I don't want to take any chances."

"I guess, now come before we be late. My cousin Donnie is already outside."

Rolling my eyes, I bumped her out of the mirror before looking down at my simple outfit. I sported a red suede skirt with a matching tube top and a pair of red custom made, high top converses. After fluffing out my curly afro, I grabbed my purse and followed Rena outside to her cousin's car. Donnie got out of his blue 2016 Honda Accord before dapping Rena up.

"Yo cus, you ain't told me your friend was banging like that!" he said while rubbing his hands together and walking towards me.

"I have a licensed gun and I know how to use it." I smiled showing him my pistol in my bag. He threw his hands up in surrender and stepped back, still checking me out from a distance.

"My bad, my bad, Rena usually be having ugly ass hood rat friends. You look completely different from them other hoes."

I laughed while Rena flipped him the bird. I rolled my eyes out of amusement watching Donnie open the door for me.

"She's not gonna give you any pussy, stop acting fake. This nigga don't ever open doors for any girl unless he want something from them" said Rena, popping him upside his head.

"Quit lying to that girl, you out here trying to make me look like a hoe. She's lying, I'm just being a gentleman."

Rena and I got in the car and the entire ride, they bickered back and forth about any and everything. As bad as Rena talked about how she was glad they were in two separate states, it was evident that they missed each other.

"Alright now, I'm not here to babysit anybody. As bad as my future baby mama is looking in the backseat, I'm not watching y'all tonight. I'll be out this bitch around twelve o'clock. Y'all got three hours to cut the fuck up and come the fuck on. I will leave y'all ass here high and dry." said Donnie pulling into the full parking lot. Killing the engine, Rena grabbed my arm and we separated from Donnie, going our separate ways.

"Okay, I'm getting a lil nervous." I said looking at the groups of people who had their eyes on us.

"Girl please, of course they're gonna act like they never seen a bad bitch before." she scoffed walking inside. *The Box* blasted through the speakers of the house while people danced, smoked, and drank.

"Girl, I'm gonna go get something to drink. I'll be right back." said Rena. I stopped her and looked at her as if she was crazy.

"I think the fuck not. We already had this conversation during the ride here. Wherever you go, I follow. Nobody finna snatch me the fuck up!"

"Okay then, come on."

We walked through the crowd of people until we finally made it to the kitchen. I groaned in annoyance when I opened the fridge and all I saw was different cases and bottles of liquor.

"Damn, they ain't got no water?" Rena and I said in unison.

We laughed at each other just for thinking alike. That was one thing I could say about her, she had her moments but when it was time to be responsible, she was on it. She didn't judge me for not being a drinker or smoker and she never judged me for being hard on her like my other so-called friends.

"You in the wrong place if you lookin for water."

Rena and I turned around and damn near stumbled back when we came face to face with the guy who was talking to us. Rena and I had two different tastes in guys, she went for the light skins and I didn't judge her preference. The fine piece of chocolate that stood in front of me caught my eyes like a main attraction. He stood at least six foot one with waves deeper than a tsunami. My eyes roamed as his muscles bulged through his red Ralph Lauren polo shirt. Rena elbowed me snapping me out of my gaze.

"Y'all kidneys gonna be fucked up with all this liquor. For real, where's the water or soda? Shit, we need something other than this." I said pointing towards the fridge.

"We got a cooler full of soda and water outside."

"Wow, well thanks." I smiled getting prepared to walk off but he stopped me.

"I've never seen you before."

"We're not from around here."

"First time in the A?"

"Well, for me it is."

"Oh, shit! Well how you liking it so far?"

"It's actually my first day here, we're here for two days."

"Oh word? Where you from though?"

"Houston."

"Ah shit, okay big Texas in the building." he laughed before taking a sip of whatever was in his red plastic cup.

"Yeah, anyways, thanks for pointing us towards proper hydration, we gotta go." said Rena pulling me.

"Damn no name?"

"I'm Rena and this is Lisa." Rena replied with a fake smile before dragging me outside.

"Damn bitch, you're rude." I laughed.

"No, I'm not, I was trying to get you away from his ass. Remember what we're here for. Remember your words."

"You act like I was gonna go upstairs and fuck home boy." I laughed.

"I know but still, we can't take any chances."

Rena and I grabbed a bottle of water before heading back inside. We talked, danced, and made videos to create memories. It was going on twelve o'clock and I was beyond tired. The entire time I was there I could feel the same guy from earlier looking at me from across the room.

"Donnie said he'll be ready in a few. You wanna go use the bathroom or grab something before we leave?" asked Rena, reading the text on her phone from Donnie.

"Yeah I'm gonna go to the bathroom, you can go ahead and meet up with Donnie and I'll text you guys when I'm done."

"I don't know, Lisa, you know I don't wanna leave you here alone."

"I'm not alone, you're here. Matter fact, you can stay right here until I get back."

"That'll work."

I nodded before walking upstairs to the bathroom. I groaned in annoyance once I'd noticed the long line at the door. I was on the verge of pissing myself if I didn't find a bathroom soon.

"You can use the one in my bedroom." said the guy from earlier, coming up behind me.

"Uh, I don't know. I can wait until they're done."

"You sure? I mean nobody ever goes in my room so you can use it if you want to." I looked at him hesitantly before finally giving in.

I didn't want to keep Donnie and Rena waiting and I knew I wasn't going to make it to the bathroom even if I tried. I reached my hand in my bag and kept it on my gun in case he tried anything with me. He was cute but he could have been dangerous for all I knew.

"I'll stand outside the room door if it makes you comfortable."

"I'll appreciate that."

He showed me to his bedroom, and I went to the bathroom that was conjoined to it. After relieving myself I pulled my phone out to call Samya, since I didn't get a chance to do so yet. Dialing her number and pressing the phone to my ear, I waited for her to answer. Since she sent me straight to voicemail, I assumed she was asleep. Opening the door, I walked out of the bathroom to be met with the guy from earlier.

"I thought you were gonna stay outside the room."

"I had to come get something." he replied digging into his dresser and pulling out a wallet.

"I guess. But thanks for letting me use your bathroom."

"No problem, I'm Tristen by the way."

"Nice meeting you Tristen, but I gotta go before my best friend run up here and put out an Amber Alert.

"True, well make sure you come and hit me up before you head back."

"I'll think about it." I smiled.

"Bye, Texas."

"Bye, Georgia." I laughed walking out the door.

Chapter 13: Shadows

Samya

"Alright, tell me what the doctor says when you guys get back." I said, while hanging out the door watching Una help my Nana in the car.

"I will. Hey, do you want anything to eat while we out?"

"Nah, I'm gonna cook."

"Oh, what you cooking?"

"That's for you to find out when you guys get back."

"Ugh okay, and make sure you call everybody and make sure they're coming to dinner tonight. You know how Nana is about her Sunday dinner."

"I got this, Una." I laughed watching her go over everything she told me in her head.

"I'm just making sure."

"If you don't bring your hind on." said my Nana, rolling down her window.

I watched as they pulled out of the yard. After they disappeared from my eyesight, I walked back inside and made my way to the kitchen. Pulling out pots and pans, I began to start my Nana's Sunday dinner, knowing she wasn't going to have the strength to do so when she came back from her doctor's appointment.

"Hey Alexa, play music on Spotify."

My music began to play throughout the house as I pulled all the food from the fridge. I began to cut up some greens and hum to the music. After four hours of cooking, beads of sweat began to trickle down my face, once I began to truly throw down in the kitchen. I smiled in accomplishment looking down at the white rice, greens, pork chops, yams, baked macaroni, cornbread, homemade BBQ chicken, corn, Pirlo rice, and red velvet cake. I was cooking for fifteen people and I was sweating like a slave in the kitchen.

It was around seven thirty and Una and my Nana still weren't back. I knew after her appointment my Nana went to visit my grandpa's grave and then she had to do something at the center. Going towards my room, I pulled out the last outfit that no one had seen me wear yet. I wasn't going to lie and say I wasn't a little down that I had to leave the next day. I was accustomed to being under my Nana and Una every day and leaving was going to bring some tears to my eyes. Especially since I knew that my Nana only had a short amount of time to live. I still couldn't believe that, and I wasn't going to be okay with that. I was so determined to call my job and quit, head home and get Jalisa and just live here.

Grabbing my nude, off the shoulder dress, a towel and wash cloth, I went to the bathroom and turned on the shower. I began to strip out of my clothes, waiting for the water to get accustomed to the temperature of my liking. Once the water reached the right temperature, I got in. After taking a fifteen-minute shower, I twisted the knob turning the water off. Sliding the glass door open, I noticed my dress was no longer in the spot I'd placed it in. Not really in the mood to play with Una, I wrapped my towel around my body and opened the door letting all the steam out.

"Una come on; I don't have time to play with you right now." I said while walking into my room.

As soon as I turned the light on, I nearly pissed myself. There was Cameron sitting on my bed holding my dress. I looked around the room for the nearest thing to defend myself with.

"Well, well, well. Long time no see, baby." he smirked standing up and placing my dress on the bed.

"If you leave now, I won't call the police." I said stepping back with every step he took closer.

"Police? That's how you treat your baby daddy? Your man? The man that helped you off the ground when you were nothing."

"Can you please leave."

"Leave for what? I just came to talk to you. I think I got the right to do so."

"Cam, I don't have shit to say to you. Get out before I call the police!"

"I ain't going nowhere until we talk." he replied, backing me into the corner. I couldn't do nothing but freeze and look up into his eyes. Those same devilish eyes that caused me so much pain and trauma.

"Talk about what?"

"About us."

"There is no fucking us!" I yelled trying to brush past him and get to my phone, but he grabbed me and shoved me back to the wall.

"Don't make me bring out the old nigga I used to be." he replied, gripping my chin and pulling me inches from his face.

"Cam please, leave." I cried.

"What you crying for? I ain't even do nothing *yet*." he said gripping my thigh.

"Because I want you to leave."

"After we discuss some business."

"Like what?"

"Where's my son? I see you've been MIA for a while now. Just to my luck, I was let out early just to come and see how you've been."

I froze like a statue when he mentioned CJ. I knew if he'd found out what happened he would kill me right here where I stood. I felt like shit for doing what I'd done, and I was scared shitless to tell this man that I'd killed his child.

"I'm waiting," he said leaning in my face.

I swallowed the lump in my throat trying to avoid eye contact with him. It felt as if even when he was in prison and I was miles away, I felt him near me. I felt him on my back waiting to hurt me and as soon as I started getting comfortable; my worst fear ended up standing right in front of me. He was like a shadow that I couldn't get rid of.

"He's with my Nana." I lied.

"Oh really?"

"Yes, he's with her."

"I can wait till he get back."

"No, you can see him tomorrow."

"I said what I said."

"Cam please, I promise you can see him tomorrow." I pleaded hoping he would just leave.

He looked down at me before gripping my ass and pulling me closer to him. I tried to keep my composure the entire time hoping he wouldn't try anything. He grabbed my chin and planted a kiss on my lips before letting me go.

"I've missed you. I'll be back tomorrow at nine." he replied, getting ready to walk out. I wiped my lips off and tightened my towel around my body. I stood closer to the glass lamp preparing to defend myself once he stopped in his tracks.

"One more thing," he said turning around to face me.

"What?"

"If you try some funny shit, I got something that'll get you straight."

"What do you mean?"

"It came to my attention that your brother is one of my known sellers. It also came to my knowledge that Teddy had to beat his ass down for not paying me my money. I mean, I don't trust him so I think I might just put a bullet in between his eyes."

"Stay the fuck away from my brother!"

"See you tomorrow." he smiled walking out of the room.

I ran to the door and locked it before throwing on a pair of sweats and an oversized T instead. Grabbing my phone from the bed I dialed Seven's number and was instantly sent to voice-mail.

"Come on Sev, please answer your phone." I panicked, pacing back and forth.

I called his phone nearly fifty times before giving up. I knew he was going to come to the house for dinner but I couldn't wait. I needed to leave and as soon as possible. Grabbing my suitcase, I threw all of my things inside and grabbed my keys. As soon as I walked out of the bedroom, I screamed when I bumped into someone. Looking up, a wave of relief washed over me seeing Jayceon standing there.

"What the fuck are you doing here?!" I yelled, running my hands through my hair in frustration.

"Damn, I can't get a hey or wassup." he laughed lightly.

"Right now, is not the time."

"I thought you were leaving tomorrow." he said looking

down at my suitcase.

"Something came up."

"Is everything okay with your sister?"

"Yes, I just have to go." I replied trying to walk past him, but he grabbed me.

"What's wrong? What happened?"

"I can't tell you."

"Look, whatever it is, you look fucking terrified. Do I gotta fuck somebody up?"

"Jay please, I have to go. Look, do me a favor and tell my Nana something urgent came up."

"Look, talk to me. I need you to calm down. I'm not lying to your grandma." He grabbed my arm, led me to the couch and sat down. He pulled me close before placing my hands in his.

"Someone I've been running away from finally found me."

"Who?"

"I can't tell you who."

"Do we need to call the police or something?"

"No Jay, it's not that simple. Look I need to go before he finds out that I'm leaving and try to follow me."

"What did he do to you that got you so shaken up?"

"I can't tell you."

"You've been telling me what's been on your mind since I've met you. Why stop now?"

"You're gonna judge me."

"Why would I judge you?"

"Because I judge myself."

"I would never judge you."

"I killed my baby." I mumbled breaking down in his arms.

He held me and let me release all of the hurt and anger I was holding in for so long. I was so hurt and mad at myself for taking my child's life away just because of the fucked-up choices I'd made. I knew from the start when I found out I was pregnant that I should have aborted him. I wasn't mentally prepared for a baby and I was already suffering from depression and being abused damn near on a daily basis.

"I loved my baby. I swear I loved him to death, I just couldn't do it anymore. I was still a fucking teenager; I didn't know how fucked up my head was. He damn near beat me to death the same day. My baby just wouldn't stop crying and crying and I couldn't take it anymore. I couldn't handle having a baby by a man who raped me and beat me. I drowned my fucking baby and let a close friend of mine take the fall for it."

"It wasn't your fault."

"It's all my fucking fault, you don't understand that?! All my life I've been blaming other people and I would never blame myself. It's my fault my fucking father left, it's my fault for everything!"

He grabbed my face and pressed his lips to mine. He pulled away before wiping my tears away with his thumb. "Don't ever blame yourself for something you aren't responsible for."

He pulled me on top of him and slipped his hands into my sweats before pressing his lips to mine. I felt his fingers spread my second set of lips. A gasp escaped my lips as he pumped both his index fingers inside of me. All the tension and hurt I was holding in suddenly vanished for just a moment when he touched me in the way he was doing.

"Fuck, Jay." I moaned aloud as his other hand gripped my breast through my shirt. Once I heard a car outside, I quickly removed his hands and stood up, drying my face.

"I think it's time for you to go."

"Me too." he replied looking down at his wedding band.

Una and my Nana came into the house and Jayceon made his way out. When Una noticed my suitcase, she pulled me to the side.

"Uh where the hell you going? I thought you were leaving tomorrow, and what is Jay fine ass doing here?"

"Something came up, I have to go."

"Something more important than spending your last day here with your family? You know Nana is gonna be pissed off."

"Cameron snuck in here and-."

"Did he fucking touch you? Did this nigga break out of fucking jail?!"

"Look, he's asking about CJ and you and I both know he will kill me if he found out what I did."

"Damn." she sighed, pulling me into a hug and rubbing circles in my back.

"He threatened to kill Seven if I don't meet with him tomorrow with CJ."

"Look, you might have to take Seven with you."

"I'm not doing that, he's not gonna come."

"How about this, since it's too risky for you to stay another night here, I'll drop Seven off Tuesday. I know you're not gonna tell him everything but listen, I will."

"No, just tell him about CJ and Cameron. What Will and mama did, I'll tell him about that."

"Okay, I got you but at least go tell Nana bye."

We shared a hug before I went to my Nana rooms to see her curling her hair. I snuck up behind her and gave her a hug, making her jump.

"What's the matter with you, child? Almost gave me a heart attack!"

"My bad, Nana."

"I hope you not wearing that to dinner?" she asked, eyeing me.

"About that."

"What's wrong?"

"Something came up with Jalisa back home, I have to leave tonight."

"No. I mean, come on Mya sweety. You said tomorrow would be your last day."

"I know but I have to get home to Jalisa. I'm sorry Nana." I replied wiping a stray tear.

This was what I was dreading the most. Say goodbye, not knowing if it was probably going to be my last goodbye. Only the Lord knew when I would be back there.

"Well if I'm still kicking, don't be a stranger. Next time bring Jalisa too, I ain't seen that girl in forever."

"Don't talk like that, I promise you I'll bring her to see you."

"Good, now go fix you a plate and get on that road." she smiled, bringing me into a hug and kissing my cheek.

"I love you, Nana."

"I love you more, baby." she smiled rocking me from side to side.

Una and my Nana walked me outside to my car the same time Will, my mom, and Seven pulled up.

"Please look out for him for me, Una." I begged really worried about what Cameron would do to him.

"I got him; I'll take him out of town for a few days just to keep things on the low."

"Thank you, I would really appreciate it.

"So, you leavin huh?" said Seven, walking over to my car.

"Sadly, yeah. As bad as I wish I could stay longer, I can't."

"It was cool while it lasted."

"Nigga how you mean? The entire time all we did was argue." I laughed lightly.

"Still, it just felt good having you here."

"Are you high?"

"No, for real though. Some crazy shit done happened to me this week and I wanna apologize to you. I was a real dick on some real shit. Jamir and a close friend of mine sat down and talked to me. I know you ain't gonna be able to do it now but hit me up when you get a chance so we can talk."

"I will." I smiled.

He reached into the car and pulled me into a hug; the first hug I'd ever gave him. For once It felt good to be in his presence without knowing we were going to argue. He pulled away before sighing as if he wanted to get in the car with me.

"You're always welcome to come to Houston anytime you want to. I'll even clear out one of my extra rooms for you."

"I'll hold you to that." he smiled.

I cranked my car up and drove away, not even staying a little longer to talk to my mom or Will. Pulling out of my cell phone, I dialed Renny's number and to my luck he answered on the third ring.

"Yes, baby mama, how may I help you?"

"I'm coming home."

Chapter 14: Sobriety

Jayceon

<u>Five Months Later</u>

"Jay stop, you know I'm tired. Your son has been kicking the fucking daylights out of me all day." said Sabrina, holding her belly.

"Any other time you like me rubbing your feet."

"I don't care, I don't want you rubbing my feet now." she replied taking her feet off my lap.

"Yeah but when you want me to eat your pussy tonight, I'm gonna tell you I'm tired too." I laughed.

"You're gonna eat this pussy regardless."

We shared a laugh before Ace's loud ass busted up in my house. I prepared myself for the argument the two were about to have. Ace and Sabrina argued like they were fucking married. We were in the midst of getting the locks changed because Ace had a key to the place in case of emergencies. Sabrina was tired of him walking in when he pleased, so she decided on getting the locks changed.

"What up, my nigga?" he said coming in the living room with Jace behind him.

"What's good?"

"He the only one you see?" asked Sabrina, giving him the side eye and sucking her teeth.

"You know I don't fucking like you." Ace replied plopping down on the couch beside us and taking the remote, changing it from what Sabrina was watching.

"You know what, you a miserable piece of shit and no bitch will ever want you. That's why you always over here in our fucking business."

"Aww poor lil stank stank! You think I give a fuck?" he laughed, kicking his feet up on the table like she was.

"Get the fuck out, nobody even invited you."

"Sorry pissy prissy, go find somebody else to play with, aight."

"Babe get your fucking friend." she snapped sitting up.

"I'm not about to start with the both of y'all today."

"I'm going to fucking bed before I beat his ass."

"And I'll wait for you to drop that baby and have my cousin beat yo ass in the streets. You swear you think you hot shit, please take your ass to sleep or something!"

Sabrina groaned before talking shit the entire time upstairs to the bedroom.

"You gonna quit talking to my wife crazy." I laughed shaking my head.

"She always come at me."

"She just wanted you to speak to her."

"Well I did, shit. What she want me to do, be her fucking best friend and paint her damn nails?" he scoffed.

I looked over at Jace, who was all in his phone since he'd come in.

"Who you texting nigga?"

"My fucking baby mama, she said my daughter got the fucking flu. I swear this one triflin bitch. How the fuck you let her get the flu and then wanna drop her off to me. Every time something going on with my child her ass wanna dump her on me. I mean I love my daughter to death but damn, man! She waits till she knows I gotta fucking work to wanna drop her off."

"We already told you to get full custody of Chastity."

"I'm trying man, but Chastity loves her bird ass mama and I don't wanna take her away. Then whenever I threaten to take full custody, her ass wanna cry. She knows she not gonna win a custody battle. Her ass still lives with her mama and she works at Wendy's."

"Damn, man." I scoffed shaking my head.

"Enough about crazy bitches. See, that's why I always wear a fucking condom. Now look at y'all dumb asses. Yo dumb ass stuck with an alcoholic, section eight, Wendy's employee, and your stupid ass stuck with a boujie, knock off, Kim K broad as a wife and had the nerve to knock her ass up again."

"Shut the fuck up!" Jace yelled, throwing a pillow at him.

"I'm tellin mama! I'm tired of you throwing shit at me and hitting me, now. You knocked my fucking earring out yesterday; I'll be wrong if I knock yo mother fucking nose, right?" Ace huffed holding his face.

"I don't give a fuck."

"Alright, enough of that shit but on some real shit, George hit me up this morning." I said trying to stop them before they started hard down, fighting in my living room.

"Talking about what?"

"His bachelor party in three days."

"Where it's gonna be at?"

"In Houston. You know his people live there."

"Oh, say word? Speaking of Houston, when was the last time you hit thickums up?" asked Ace, rubbing his hands together with a smirk as he referred to Samya.

"I ain't talk to her since she left, and imma keep it that way."

The night that I'd gone to her grandmother's house to drop something off, I didn't expect for her to be in the state of mind she was in. It was an instinct of mine to make her tell me what was on her mind because I did that for a living. I was so used to helping people who seemed off their shit, that I didn't even notice I wasn't treating her like a patient. I was treating her like she was something more to me.

Ever since she'd first arrived, it was something about her. Her aura, her energy, everything just seemed to attract me to her. I knew it was wrong for me to act the way I did whenever I was around her because I was married to Sabrina. I gave Sabrina every reason to trust me and I slipped up onetime jeopardizing that. There I was getting a second chance at protecting my marriage; another chance to restart my family that was once broken and was ready to risk it all for a girl I'd only known for almost a week.

"Damn, lil baby must have broken your heart." laughed Ace.

"She ain't did shit, y'all must have forgotten I'm married."

"Nigga please, Sabrina cheated on your ass four times and you still with her ass. Nigga you can slip up once."

"That was then, this is now. That was when we first lost Micah. We both weren't on our shit. I mean, I would drink my day away while she would run away and cope in a different way. Being sober now makes me look back on how fucked up I was then."

"Speaking of Micah, how y'all holding up?" asked Jace.

"I tried to get her to decide on cleaning out his room so we can make it into the new baby's room but she's not having it. I mean she'll go into his room in the middle of the night and sit in there and cry. I don't see the point of cleaning out my office and making that into the baby room."

"She still trying to cope with it."

"I see that but still, she walks by his room every day as if he's still here. I ain't even finna lie and say I ain't worried about her."

"Just clean it out while she's out with her friends or something. I mean she'll be aight."

"I thought about doing that, but it's not just my decision."

"I know but think about this. Would you rather her be depressed her entire pregnancy knowing that she got her deceased son's belongings in the room across the hall, or would you rather get rid of all that shit for the both of you to finally get that weight lifted off your shoulders?"

"I'll think about it, man." I sighed, looking down at Micah's name tattooed on my wrist.

"But you going to Houston?" Asked Jace.

"I don't know, I might."

"Y'all niggas wanna carpool?" asked Ace. "It don't make sense for all of us to take three different cars."

"We can do that, I just gotta call my sister up to keep Sabrina company until I get back. She don't like being here by herself at night."

"You making her bean head ass sound like a fucking child."

"Nah for real, It's something about being here at night by herself that drives her crazy. That's another reason why I wanna clear that room out."

"But what about yo fine ass sister, ask her why she ain't hit me up."

"Ace, my sister is in a fucking relationship. When her nigga come over and bust a cap in yo ass I don't wanna hear shit."

"I shoot nigga's too! The fuck I look like, Bobo the fool? Your sister wants me, she just don't know it yet." he laughed.

"You need to find you a bitch and ASAP, because I'm tired of you coming for my sisters and cousins."

"I'll come for your mama too, with her fine ass."

"Get yo ass beat the fuck up if you want to." I replied, giving him the side eye.

"I was just playin, my nigga. But on some real shit, I don't know about y'all but I'm finna pack my three day bag for this lil trip and buy me up some condoms, cause like I mentioned before, I wrap it up unlike y'all." laughed Ace, rubbing his hands together.

Chapter 15: The All Knowing

Samya

"Yes bitch, show me face and ass." said Renny, while snapping photos of me for my website.

I'd just had a very important business meeting about opening up my own shop. I'd always had a dream to have my own shop where I hired artists of every kind, to showcase their art along with mine. I had a whole book full of ideas for my shop. Sip and paint, art lessons, fundraisers, and many more. I even thought about adding Jalisa's ideas in on my plan.

"Okay that's enough, and don't act all cool with me now because I'm still mad at you." I said while sitting down.

"I said I'm sorry. Look, Jalisa is grown and she came back perfectly fine."

"That's the thing though, what if she didn't?"

"But she did! She came back okay, and she had a good time. You need to let her go out more often, hun. She even came back with so many stories to tell."

"I do let her go out, I let her go anywhere she wanna go. But one thing that pissed me off with you was I trusted you, Renny, to keep an eye on her and you fucking let her go all the way to Atlanta. somewhere she has never been but once and that was with me. I don't give a fuck if she was going there because God himself told her to go. That's my sister and she's like a daughter to me."

"I understand that completely and I was wrong for not calling you. I should have never given her the okay to go."

"Just don't let it happen again, okay Renny?"

"I won't." he replied sitting beside me and hugging me.

"Now get off me before I cut you off." I laughed.

"You could never find another bitch like me." he replied, elbowing me.

"Yeah whatever. Maybe in the next three months, I'm gonna need you to go to Jonesboro for me."

"Of course, what you need me to go down there for?"

"Well my brother Seven and his girlfriend been there for a few months now."

"Still hiding from your crazy ass ex?"

"Pretty much, but I'm low on money now and I can't afford to keep paying for their rent and everything anymore. So, they're going to live with me until they get back on their feet."

"Ain't his lil girlfriend pregnant?"

"Yes, she is, and she's one of the artists I'm gonna hire to work at my shop. Her work is amazing, trust me you'll love it."

"Oh okay, well sure I can get them. I had a lil boo thing back in Arkansas, shit I might stop and get that." he laughed.

"I guess, but how are you doing though?" he asked, referring to my therapy session.

When I came back home, I decided on starting my therapy sessions again. For the most part everything was going pretty well, and I actually felt like I didn't have to look over my shoulder anymore. I hadn't heard from Cam since I'd left and it was to the point where if I did see him, I wouldn't be the same person I was before. The girl who would be scared just from the sound of his voice, was gone.

"I'm doing a lot better. I actually feel good. I feel like a weight has been lifted off my shoulder and I'm no longer this scared girl I used to be. My depression is no longer with me anymore, you know? I don't feel that shadow over my shoulder that I'd been feeling for the longest."

"I'm proud of you." he smiled.

"I'm proud of myself."

"That's good, but anyways I noticed that lady been staring you down ever since we got here. I just didn't wanna say anything, but if she keeps looking I'm gonna knock her wig straight."

I turned my head in the direction he was looking before I noticed who he was talking about. A smile spread across my face when I locked eyes with Spice. I stood up and walked over to her with Renny hot on my trail.

"Spice?"

"Well, well, well, if it ain't, Babydoll." she replied getting up from her seat.

"I don't go by that anymore."

"Hm, you used to love that name. I was the one who gave it to you."

"That was then." I shrugged.

"Hmm, and what you doing now?"

"I own a business. What do you do?"

"I'm a bartender at the club."

"Still there I see."

"Yup, money still good."

"I bet." I laughed lightly.

"Yeah, Vince retired and moved up North. His brother owns this business now."

"Hm, that's good. Would have thought you would retire by now. Aren't you in your forties?"

"Forty-five and don't look it." she smiled, flipping her bundles.

"Hm, yeah right."

"Ever thought about coming back? The new girls couldn't do it like you did on your first night."

"Hold up, bitch you used to strip?" asked Renny, with a raised eyebrow.

"The best damn stripper in Houston! Tell him, Babydoll, you had niggas coming from all over. In fact, that was how she met her lil boo thang Cameron." she smiled.

"I thought your ex was from Baton Rouge like you?" questioned Renny confused.

"He was, but his brother lived here at the time."

"Oh okay, but when the hell were you were going to tell me that you used to strip?" Renny replied with his arms crossed.

"I didn't think it was something I had to share."

"Well, you were the best of the best; that's something to brag about. You know you're always welcome back."

"Why would I come back?"

"For some quick money of course."

"I don't know, Spice."

"Come on, Babydoll."

"It's Samya. At least act like you remember that."

"I think I like Babydoll better." she smiled.

"I don't care what you like better. You know my name so act like you know."

"Hm, attitude?"

"You damn skippy."

"If you ever change your mind, just know Eddie still is a bodyguard; I'm sure he'll remember you. Just request a song and get up on stage, babe. I'll even talk to Vincent's brother to let him know you might come."

"Don't waste your breath."

"Just think about it. Bye Babydoll," she smiled, walking off towards her car.

"So, you was a stripper?"

"Yes, Renny, damn!"

"Uh uh, don't raise your voice at me bitch."

I ignored his remarks once I heard my cellphone ringing. Pulling it out, I saw Seven's name flash across the screen. Answering the phone, I pressed it to my ear.

"Wassup."

"Look, I need you to come get me and Mariah now!"

"What's wrong? What's going on? Are you okay? Is the baby okay?"

"Teddy been snooping around; I think he knows we here. Look, I need you to come and get me as soon as possible. I thought we could lay low longer, but I can't."

"Okay, calm down. I'll get my friend Renny to come and get you guys first thing tomorrow, okay? Whatever you do, just don't leave the house."

"Aight, just hurry up okay. I don't give a fuck about what happens to me, but I don't know what I'll do if something happens to Mariah and our baby, man."

"Nothing is going to happen to you guys, I promise, okay?"

"Alright, I'll hit you up later."

"Alright, love you and be safe, please."

"I love you too." he replied clicking over.

"Renny, I might have to push that date a lot closer. I need you to go get them first thing tomorrow, please."

"I have to go visit my grandmother. I can do it the day after."

"That'll work."

"Okay but when I come back tomorrow, I wanna see your ass at the club."

"I'm not going back to that club."

"Why not? I mean, didn't you just say that you needed the money. At least make that fast money for one night. And didn't Salt Shaker say you were good?"

"Her name is Spice." I laughed.

"As I was saying, didn't Black Pepper say were good?"

"I was, but still."

"Come on, one night, tomorrow night."

"Fine, just so I can get a lil cash to pay for my building."

"Thank you." he jumped around in excitement.

"What the hell you so excited about?"

"Because I get to see my best friend shake some ass and get some cash!" he yelled with his tongue out.

"Yeah whatever, let's go."

Renny and I got into my car and drove straight to my house.

"Did you notice Jalisa's acting a lil off?" I asked.

"I mean, she always acts weird. You gotta be more specific than that."

"Every time I come home, she goes to her room and ignores me."

"I mean you chewed her the fuck out when she came back from Atlanta. You were real harsh on her, you called her a bitch and all."

"You knew what I was going through, Renny."

"I know but still, it doesn't help the fact she had to settle for community college."

"She still didn't tell me why." I sighed, shaking my head.

"Just give her a chance."

"It's been five months since we've had that argument and she's walking around like I fucking killed her dog. I don't know what the fuck has gotten into her but I'm trying the best I can."

"You're right about one thing, she couldn't shut up about wanting to go to Spelman and now she's settling for community college?"

"I just don't know man. Something is off and I'm gonna find out, I know that."

"I doubt it's anything big, you know how Jalisa gets."

"I guess." I replied, pulling into my driveway. Pulling the keys from the ignition, I prepared myself for this conversation with Jalisa.

"One more thing," said Renny stopping me from getting out the car.

"What?"

"You need to tell her you went back home. That's the least you can do, Mya.

"I can never find the time to tell her."

"How about you tell her now. You had no right to get on her ass for going out and not telling you, while you went back home to see family she hasn't seen since she was twelve."

"Don't do that."

"I am doing this. Now you go in that house and make that the first thing you tell her."

I couldn't even sit there and argue with Renny because I knew he was right. Jalisa was eighteen and I still hid shit from her as if she was still a child. I wasn't hiding my little sister from the world; I was hiding the world from her. Jalisa was smart, determined, and she was dedicated in life. I felt like a proud big sister because I raised her right and she could never do any wrong. She was more worried about getting good grades and going to college to follow her dreams, than going out there doing crazy shit and getting knocked up like the other group of people she hung around. People tried to persuade her to do the wrong thing, when she knew not to.

"I'll tell her."

"Good, I'll be right by your side like always." he smiled.

Jalisa

"Come on man, you gotta tell her." said Rena, stroking my hair as I laid in her lap.

"I can't." I sniffled.

"Well, for the past three months you've been crying to me about it. I already told you to call the fucking police."

"You know I can't do that. I already told you what he said."

"Well you can't just sneak behind your sister's back and get an abortion."

"I can't have this baby, Rena." I cried into her lap.

"Look, your starting to show and the more you wait, the less time you're gonna have to be able to get an abortion. You have to tell Samya."

"She's already disappointed in me, Rena."

"No, she's not."

"Yes, she is. I was supposed to be better than this. I was supposed to go to Spelman and become an author. Now look at me!" I cried.

"The more you blame yourself it's gonna make me blame myself. If it wasn't for me pushing the idea up in your head, we would have never gone to Atlanta." Rena sniffled.

I held onto her as we cried together. There I was blaming myself for what happened to me and she blamed herself. I quickly dried my face when I heard the front door open.

"Tell her please." begged Rena.

"Promise you're gonna be by my side the whole way."

"I promise." she replied holding out her pinky.

I intertwined my pinky with hers before we walked out the door hand in hand. Looking over the staircase watching Renny and Mya walk through the door laughing. I felt Rena grip my hand for comfort before we made our way downstairs. Renny and Mya's attention landed on us, giving us a look of worry. I assumed it was because of our red, puffy eyes.

"Everything okay?" Samya asked while walking over and pulling me into a hug. Just from her hugging me, I felt the tears coming. I broke down crying on her shoulder.

"I'm sorry." I cried.

"Sis we argue all the time, it's not that deep to cry about." she laughed, rubbing my back.

"No, It's something else."

She pulled away before looking at Renny and Rena, indicating that she needed privacy. I grabbed Rena's hand not wanting to have to tell Samya the news alone.

"No, I want them here." I said while grabbing her hand and sitting down on the couch.

"What's going on?" she asked again, holding onto my shaking hands.

"I'm pregnant." I cried holding my head down.

I didn't want to see the look on her face. The look of disappointment that I hated so bad. I hated to see her and Renny look at me as if I was the biggest disappointment in the world.

"Lift your head up." Said Renny, kneeling down in front of me and wiping my eyes.

"I'm not mad at you, neither am I disappointed." said Mya, pulling me into her arms.

"Tell them, Lisa." said Rena.

"When we were in Atlanta we went to this party. Even though we were only down there for two days, I met this guy. He was sweet and I thought he was cool, so I gave him my number. I told him where I lived and everything. I needed someone to vent to, you know? You were either always working or you had your own issues. He listened to me and after a month of talking, he road down here with Donnie and we hung out. While you were at work, he broke in and he-." I couldn't even finish before I fully broke out in tears, imagining what he'd done to me. I looked up at Samya who was now in tears herself.

"I'm sorry." she said, pulling me into her arms and rocking me back and forth.

"It's all my fault. I should have never went to Atlanta."

"It's not your fault, stop it. Look, we have to call the police."

"No! We can't do that!"

"Why! He fucking raped you, Lisa!" she yelled.

"He knew you! He knows who you are! He said that Cameron sent him! He said if I call the police, you will be next." I cried in her chest.

"I don't give a fuck about what happens to me! You're my fucking life, Jalisa! I don't give a fuck if they threatened to fucking put a bullet in my head! You protect your fucking self you hear me!"

"I'm sorry."

"How far along are you?"

"Three months."

"Renny, can you stay with her real fast? I need a minute." said Samya, getting up from the chair and walking outside. Renny sat next to me and let me cry myself to sleep in his arms.

Chapter 16: Pretty Bird

Samya

"How you holding up?" asked Renny, sprawled out on my bed passing me the blunt.

"I feel like shit. It's like whenever I think I'm getting into a good place in my life, something has to come in and fuck it up, you know?"

"So, what you gonna do?"

"What the fuck can I do, Ren. I was so fucking caught up into getting clarity and trying to prove myself to my family, that I wasn't there for the only person who was there with me in the beginning." I replied, taking a long pull from the blunt.

"It's not your fault. You can't help everybody, babe."

"It's just I wanna move away with my sister again but I'm so fucking tired of running, Ren."

"Then stay and fight."

"I can't fight anymore. If I was here with Jalisa this probably wouldn't have happened. I just don't want my sister to go through what the fuck I went through. I know how it feels to be in her shoes and to feel like you have a limitation on life. It's gonna be hard to take care of a baby that you know wasn't conceived in the right way."

"She'll get through it. She got one hell of a sister to help her get through it. When you told me everything that happened to you, I was thinking, *damn I probably would have given up a while ago.*"

"Till this day, I still wanna give up you know? I've ran from this man for so long and now that I know he's free and that he could do harm, there's a part of me that wants to run like I've been doing. If he got someone to rape my sister, he knows where I live. As bad as I don't wanna move, I have to. Ren he's after my brother, my sister, and me. I can't go to Jamir because I know he will risk it all. He has a family and I don't want him to go to jail."

"You have to take it one day at a time, babe. I know it's hard, trust me."

"I finally made up my mind."

"About what?"

"Dancing tomorrow night at the club."

"Why? I would have thought you would have changed your mind after what just happened."

"Rena can stay and keep her company. I'm only dancing for one night and one night only."

"Why the change of heart though?"

"Whenever I was going through shit, on my worst days I would come to the club and dance my heart away. It was like my sanctuary when I needed some place to find myself." I replied passing him the blunt and walking over to the closet.

Pulling out a box of old stuff, I sat down on my bed and took the top off. Pulling out my mask, I smiled weakly thinking back to those days where I was Babydoll, the famous face of Candyland. The girl who had damn near fifty private dance requests each night.

"Renny, meet Babydoll." I laughed lightly, giving him the custom-made mask. I felt the high and we were only on our third blunt.

"Oh Babydoll, I like that." he coughed.

"Thank Spice, no in your words, Black Pepper came up with it." I laughed.

"I swear I love you and you're my best friend." he cried.

"This why I can't smoke with you, emotional ass." I laughed taking the blunt from his hands and putting it in the ashtray.

"But what you gonna do though? About Cameron?"

"I'm gonna fucking kill him."

After Renny went home I made my way to Jalisa's room. Opening her door, she was snuggled up against her pillow looking at the walls. Tightening my robe, I got in bed with her and placed my hand in hers.

"How you holding up, sis? You always ask me, and I barely ever ask you."

"Could be better." she sniffled, turning around to face me.

"Stop crying. Just answer me this; do you really want to keep this baby?"

"I do."

"Are you sure? Because adoption is always an option."

"No. At first I wanted an abortion I'm not even going to lie to you, but I wanted one because I was scared to disappoint you. I was scared that I'd let you down when you have all this faith and hope in me."

"You could never disappoint me. No matter what you do, you couldn't disappoint me even if you tried to. I know I put a lot on you to be a better person than I was, but I will never force you to become somebody you're not. You're liable to make mistakes because we all do. We all make mistakes and that's okay. If you want to keep this baby, I'll be right by your side through the whole thing."

"I do want to keep it."

"Well, I'm here."

"I'm gonna be a better mother to my child than our mother ever was to us."

"I believe in you." I smiled placing my hand on her little pudge that was coming in.

"Thanks for always believing in me whenever I felt like no one else was."

I fell asleep next to Jalisa, snuggled up close not wanting her out of my sight; the same feeling I had when she was younger, and we shared a bed each night. I was even hesitant to leave her home alone. Deep down inside, a part of me blamed myself and once I got my siblings in a safe space, I was gonna handle Cameron even if it killed me.

Jayceon

"Babe how long you gonna be gone?" Asked Sabrina, clinging onto me.

"I'm gonna be there for three days, no longer than that."

"That's too much, especially for a damn bachelor party." She mumbled.

"Look, we gotta head out. Baby I'll text you when I get there."

"You better." She replied, pecking my lips.

"I love you."

"I love you too. Lauren take care of my baby."

"I got this, don't go to Houston acting single." My sister, Lauren, replied giving me a firm look.

"Why would I do that?"

"Lauren, I'm still single baby but you can change that, all you gotta do is say the words and I'll go to Houston a taken man." Said Ace, sticking his head out the window.

"Listen here Benjamin, I'm not about to play with you." replied my sister calling him by his first name.

"Everybody ain't need to know my first name like that." he scoffed, sticking his head back in the car and rolling his window up. I gave Sabrina and Lauren a hug goodbye before getting into the driver's seat and pulling off.

"Yo, I meant to tell you Seven been trying to get in touch with you." said Jace, leaning back in the passenger seat.

"For what? He just stopped coming to the center a few months back and now he wanna hit me up?"

"That kid got real issues."

"You see who he hangs with, obviously he's gonna have some issues. I try my best to help him out."

"I think you give that kid way more attention than you give everybody else."

"Because I used to be like him when I was younger. I used to think nobody could tell me shit and I thought the fucking world owed me something. Seven is like a son to me and whenever he needed something, I was there."

"So why are you ignoring him?" asked Ace, popping a Dorito in his mouth.

"Because he only calls whenever he wants money. I feel like he was using me, his fucking pops got him like that. Listen, I would never abandon him, he's always welcome to come back to the center but one thing I won't do is kiss his ass and let him use me. It's like him and his damn sister are just alike. They lash out on you whenever you try to help, and I don't have time for that shit."

"Shit, I understand where you're coming from." Jace replied, shaking his head.

"Yeah man, I put too much on the line when I'm around that kid. Sabrina made me realize that. You know one time, he robbed somebody's fucking house and I let him hide out in my place for a whole two months."

"Did he ever get caught?"

"No, I got my uncle to pull some strings."

"Damn, but for the most part, it looks like you still care about him. I don't give a fuck what Sabrina say, don't let her make choices in your life like she's been doing for the longest. Especially something like this. You really care about the kids that come into your center, and just because Sabrina duck mouth ass feels some type of way about it, oh fucking well! You need to man the fuck up and stop taking orders from her ass." Ace seethed.

Ace may have had his moments when it came to Sabrina, but this was my first time seeing him genuinely pissed off. It was no secret that I treated the kids at the center like a family to me and for me to cut Seven off like I'd done was unusual for them. It seemed as if Ace had even grown close to Seven at some point, so I knew him finding out what I'd done to him, pissed him off to the core.

"Yeah man, you don't know it might be important. Just call him and check on him." Said Jace, defending Ace's case.

"Alright, whenever I get some time, I'll call him."

"Nigga we got a long ass ride ahead of us. We got nothing but time right now."

"I said I'll call when I get time."

Jace was right, I had a lot of time the entire time I was driving. I was just hiding the fact that they were right. Ever since Sabrina and I got back on the right track, I was trying to keep us on the right track. I'd invested so much time and energy into my marriage that I tried everything in my power to keep it strong. Even when we were on the verge of a divorce and we lived in separate houses, she always found it in her power to check up on me and it was the other way around. Sabrina was there for me when I was at my worst and now that we're getting a second chance at fixing our relationship, I didn't want to stir up any arguments or misconceptions with her.

The entire ride, I felt them judging me. Ace would make smart remarks or time would surpass while we sat in silence.

Chapter 17: Memories Back Then

Samya

"So, when are you going to start thinking of names?" I asked Jalisa, watching her look into the mirror trying on clothes.

"I already thought of some."

"Oh really? Okay lay them on me."

"I was thinking for a girl, I was gonna use Nana's name."

"Gale? I mean I like it, but it seems a little old fashioned."

"No, I mean her middle name. I always liked Arimona.

"I like that too, but what if it's a boy."

"Legend."

"That's cute too, I like that." I smiled.

I was happy that she was finally getting back to herself. She'd even made the choice to get her Bachelor's at our community college. The only thing I was worried about at the moment was her mentality. I wanted her to go see a therapist because when I went through what she was going through, I was traumatized. Even though I trusted her judgement when she told me she was okay, a part of me felt like she was lying.

"So, are you ready for your doctor's appointment tomorrow to find out the gender?"

"That's if they can. Hopefully I can find out tomorrow so I can finally start buying stuff." she smiled, looking down at her belly.

"You're excited?"

"Yeah, I am. At first, I was scared and didn't know what to do but thanks to you, I have a completely different look on this."

"I'm glad you feel that way. But I'm going to head out, I'll be back in at eleven, I promise."

"Oh yeah, I forgot you're going back to the club."

"Yeah, I am. Just for one night and one night only."

"I thought you said you were never going back to the club no matter what?"

"I wasn't but something came up."

"Like what? You know I hate when you don't fill me in on things."

I sighed running my hands through my hair, hesitant on what I wanted to fill her in on. She still didn't know I went to Baton Rouge and that was one thing I wanted to get off my chest. It seemed like it was never the right time to tell her. Everything that had been going on with Seven, I never told her about. I never told her anything and I knew sooner or later it was going to push her away from me.

"I have something to tell you that I should have told you in the first place."

"I'm listening."

Before I could get the words out of my mouth, I heard knocking. Well more like banging on my door. Jalisa and I gave each other a disquiet look before I walked to her closet and grabbed her metal baseball bat.

"Stay up here, I'll be right back."

She nodded watching me walk out of her room. Walking down my spiral staircase, I slowly crept up to the front door as the banging grew louder.

"Who is it!" I yelled.

Looking through the peephole, I saw that they were covering it. Preparing to beat the living daylights out of whoever was banging on my door, I placed my hand on the knob and swung it open. I raised an eyebrow in confusion looking at my mother who held a vexed expression. Before I could ask her what she was doing here, she pushed past me and walked inside.

"I should whip yo ass, you know that right?" she scoffed with her arms crossed.

"What are you talking about? And why the fuck are you here? How do you know where I stay?" I asked returning the same attitude she was giving me. She may have been my mother, but she wasn't going to come up in my house and slander threats as if she had the mother of the year award.

"Don't worry about that, but I know what the fuck we can worry about; you dirty bitch! See I tried my best to keep my composure but you, you are the fucking spawn of the devil! You thought you could fucking strut your way back home and turn my mother against me, and my fucking son?!" she yelled stepping closer as if she wanted to hit me.

I'd had to deal with people beating my ass my entire life and I'd be damned if I sat here and let her barge into my sanctuary, threatening to put her hands on me. I gripped my bat in my hand, preparing to whip her ass and if Will was outside, I was going to beat the shit out of him too.

"First of all, what the fuck you not gonna do is barge into my damn house and act like you run shit here because you don't! I told your fucking son the truth! I told my grandmother the fucking truth! You're a disgrace for a fucking parent and here I was stressing myself out trying to figure out how I could fix things, how the fuck I could get an answer!"

"Oh please. So, you think because you're, miles away from home and making money out the ass that I'm supposed to be phased by you? Up in here living good, living life with no fucking worries while your family is back home struggling. Did you know that we have a foreclosure on the house? You were always so fucking ungrateful." She scoffed.

"You're not about to do that. You're not about to guilt trip me. You put me out on the streets when I was fucking seventeen with your child; seventeen, mama! We stayed with Nana for three months before I begged Aunt Sasha to take us. We lived in a fucking shelter for months before I had to make some shit shake. All because you couldn't face the fact that your sick ass husband was praying on your youngest daughter. All because I stood up for myself because you couldn't! You think just because you my damn mama, that I'm supposed to give you everything that I have. Y'all can live on the fucking streets before I care."

"Still selfish like your fucking father! You're one ungrateful bitch and I should have aborted you when I had the chance!"

"Oh please, I hope you had the same energy for the other kids you were pregnant with. Oh yeah, I forgot William was too busy beating your ass and he killed them for you!"

I felt her hand connect with my face and it stung like fire. I gripped the bat in my hand about to swing on her until I heard Jalisa's voice.

"Mya, who's at the door?" she yelled from her room. I looked at my mother with a clenched jaw before clearing my throat.

"It's nobody, I'll be up in a minute.

"Is that my daughter?"

"It's time for you to go."

"Not without speaking to my child, I'm not." she replied trying to go upstairs.

"I said get out!"

"Jalisa?! Jalisa, baby, come downstairs it's your mama!" she yelled running up the stairs.

I ran behind her, not wanting them to see each other. Especially in the state Jalisa was in. I tried to drag her back, but it was too late. Jalisa was already standing at the top of the stairs.

"Mama?" she asked with a raised eyebrow, trying to figure out if she was really seeing what she was seeing.

"She was just leaving, Lisa." I said, in the midst of trying to pull her out of my house. She yanked away from me and walked up the stairs to get closer to Jalisa. I followed behind her getting ready to drag her down the stairs.

"What do you want?" asked Jalisa.

"I'm here to see my child of course."

"Hm, you're here to see me now after all this time, I find that funny." she ridiculed.

"I've been busy."

"Of course, you were but now that you've seen me, you can go now."

"That's how you're gonna act?"

"How do you expect me to act, ma?"

"I see your sister got you giving people the same nasty ass attitude she gives people."

"My sister did a better job raising me than you did, too. Let's not forget to give her credit where it's due."

"Wow. If that's how you feel. But baby I'm better now."

"Okay, and?"

"And I think it's time you finally come back home."

I looked at my mother as if she was crazy. Her and I would be hard on fighting if she thought I'd sit there and let her take Jalisa out of my house.

"You must still be smoking crack to think I'm gonna let you take her from me." I said stepping in front of her.

"Oh please, and your raising her better? Look at her, she's already pregnant and she's only eighteen. You probably have the nappy head ass lil boy running through your house day in and day out."

"At least I have a house that's fully paid for, for starters and I think it's best that you mind your business."

"I think it's funny how you're brainwashing my daughter to hate her own family."

"You know you're crazy right? Stop trying to pin your wrong doings on me, because it's not working. You need to know that you're not the victim in this, ma. We are! We're the fucking victims because your head is stuck so far up your ass, that you can't see what you did to us!"

"So, you're the victim, right? You've been through so much? But you came back home in the end. The home that caused you so much sorrow. Samya you're full of shit!"

"What is she talking about, Mya?" asked Jalisa.

"Oh, she didn't tell you? That explains a lot."

"Mya what is she talking about?"

"She came back home without bringing you. She was there for an entire week, you know? I was just wondering, where you were when she was there."

"I was gonna tell you bu-." I was cut off by her running into her room.

"You need to go before I call the police."

"I'm so scared." she laughed lightly, before making her way

out. After she left, I closed and locked the door behind her. Rushing upstairs, I attempted to open Jalisa's room door, but she had it locked.

"Lisa, I was gonna tell you."

"Yeah right. Listen go to the club like you say you were gonna do; Bye Mya." she replied completely shutting me out.

As soon as I'd heard her music being cranked up loud, I knew she was done talking to me. Quickly drying my eyes, I shot Rena a text and grabbed my purse. After putting the security code in, I walked out and went to my car. It took me around thirty minutes to get to the club. Pulling up, I noticed Spice wasn't lying; the club was jumping and it had more improvements than it did before. There were even renovations added on to make it three stories high. I was impressed at the most.

After parking my car near Spices white Acura, I got out with my duffle bag in tow. Approaching the crowded door, I was met with Eddie.

"Babydoll, is that you?" he asked, walking towards me.

"In the flesh." I laughed.

"Damn man, you look amazing. What you doin here?" he asked pulling me into a hug.

"Spice told me you guys were gonna be busy this week. So, I thought I'd drop by and make a lil reappearance."

"You fucking serious right now?"

"Yeah."

"Damn man, you're gonna take everybody's money. The new girls, the old girls, they just don't know what they're in for." he laughed.

"I don't know about all that now, I doubt I barely still have it."

"Man please, you used to have me giving you my paycheck

and I'm a married man."

"Stop giving me so much credit, I just went with the flow of things."

"So, you gonna go with the flow of things tonight and body every single bitch in the club?"

"Stop it. I see you still my number one fan."

"I'll always be that. You were always like a lil sister to me when you used to work here. To be honest I think you were the only one who was here with good intentions."

"Well thanks, Eddie. I'm gonna get going."

"See you on the stage, Babydoll." he smiled pulling me into another hug.

He held the door open for me and as soon as I stepped foot inside, I was astonished by the new look of things. It didn't even look anywhere near how it used to look back when I was working there. The silver poles were either gold, black, or covered in some type of material that made it sparkle like a disco ball.

"Yo, babydoll!" I turned around to see where my name was being called.

As bad as I didn't want to be called that, I couldn't get away from it being there again. Walking towards the bar, I saw Spice mixing drinks and taking money from the bar guest.

"I thought you were never gonna show up." she said stepping around the bar and pulling me into a hug.

"I told you I would think about."

"After two days of thinking?"

"You know I hate being rushed."

"Mmhm, well the changing room is upstairs."

"I'll go to the bathroom and change; I don't want to have to slap a bitch silly for no reason tonight. You know how they get when they see new faces."

"I know, but Monti knows your here. He said just go request a song and give them your name and your set."

"Oh okay." I replied preparing to walk off but she grabbed my arm.

"It's nice having you back here." she smiled.

"It's nice being back."

I walked towards the bathroom and locked the door, pulling out my attire for the night. I put on my red lace lingerie that had rhinestones decorating the bottom half, and a diamond bralette chain sparkling on the top. Unbraiding my hair, I fluffed it out giving it a more, curly look. For my final piece I put on my red lace up heels. After adding on my silver hoops, I walked out towards the mirror and looked at myself, a tad bit disappointed that I was back there. Staring into the mirror, my 17-year old self stared back at me.

"Only for one night." I said to myself looking into the mirror closer, applying a coat of sparkly lip gloss to my lips.

Pulling out my sparkling rhinestone face mask I wore every time, I placed it over my eyes. Grabbing my bag of clothes, I walked out and the room seemed more crowded than it was before I'd first come in. Giving Spice my bag of clothes, I walked up towards the Dj stand and waited for him to finish talking to one of the girls who'd just gotten off the stage. Once he noticed me, he gave me his undivided attention.

"You must be the infamous Babydoll I used to hear all about." he said rubbing his hands together. It was evident that everyone knew of Babydoll because I was the only stripper who wore a mask.

"That's me." I smiled.

"Damn, you look good too." he smirked licking his lips, looking me up and down.

"Thanks."

"So, what you wanna dance to?"

"Complexities by Daniel Caesar."

He nodded before gesturing me to walk to the stage. Going to the stage I looked up at the crowd of men, and the many more that were pulling in by the minute. I looked down at my half, exposed body before closing my eyes to take me to that happy place in my mind.

"Alright everybody, we got somebody special in here for y'all tonight. She's new but she not new. Give it up for the one and only, Babydoll!" yelled the DJ.

Opening my eyes, I gripped the pole and walked around it in circles seductively. I looked around the room to see men eyes filled with lust and I'd barely even started yet before money started flowing in. Whipping my hair to the side, I moved my ass to the beat of the song before slowly dropping down in front of the pole. I extend one of my legs, still dipped low, showing off my glistening legs that were oiled up. Slowly standing back up, I turned my back to the crowd giving them a full view of my ass as it moved every time. Twirling around the pole with my legs in the air, I slowly slid down in a split making the crowd go wild.

Money was raining down on me like a storm. Lying down on my back, I hiked my body weight up on my shoulders and opened my legs up to the sky. I laughed at the many hoots and hollers I received from the strippers along with Spice's loud-mouth in the crowd. I slowly turned around and crawled seductively to the end of the stage and teased the crowd, slowly sliding my bra strap down. One thing I didn't do was get completely naked on stage and it still astonished me to this day that I made more money than half the girls in there that were getting fully naked on demand. As soon as the song was coming to an end, I strutted towards the pole and placed my back against it, before sliding down slowly into a split.

"That's my mother fucking best friend!" yelled Renny, among the crowd of others.

I ran my fingers through my hair and ran my other hand from my stomach to my mouth. One thing that got the crowd anticipated, was me pretending to take off my mask, which I didn't. Once the song was over, Eddie had to help me fill up two large trash bags full of money. For some reason, I felt alive. I felt energetic and all the shit that was going through my mind before, was all gone. That was the only thing I enjoyed when I used to come there. All my problems suddenly vanished when I danced on stage. Memories from back then flashed through my mind like a flood and it felt good.

"Yo, I gotta get a dance from her ASAP." said Ace, watching the girl get off the stage with bags full of money.

"Me too nigga, damn she bad." said Jace, pulling out more money.

I was too busy looking at her mask and watching her movement. As soon as they said Babydoll, a flashback hit me like a brick. She was the same girl I'd met back then when I'd first lost Micah. She was the one I'd almost risked it all for. A part of me wanted to request a private dance just so I could ask her if she remembered me. The man I was now just wanted to let her go.

"Y'all want me to ask her to come over here and dance?" asked George, pulling out cash as well.

"Hell yeah."

"Who's gonna ask though? She got that big ass bodyguard following her around." said Ace.

"I'll ask." I replied getting up. I spotted her laughing and talking to the bartender. Walking over, as soon as I was close enough, the bodyguard stepped in front of me.

"What can I do for you?" he asked with his arms crossed.

"Yeah, we wanna request a dance from her." I said pointing behind him.

"So does every other guy in the building but she's not taking requests."

"Why not?"

"Because this is her one and only night and she's leaving soon."

"Damn, aight." I replied giving her one last look. I walked back over to the guys who were already being entertained by another stripper.

"She's not taking request." I said making them all groan.

"Damn." said Ace, looking over at her.

I couldn't help but to bring my attention to her too. The way the red set complimented her light skin complexion, as her rhinestones and mask glistened in the light; she was for sure something to look at. She was thick in all the right places and even though you could barely see her face, everything about her screamed sex appeal.

Once I noticed her walking towards the bathroom, I placed my beer on the table in front of me and followed her. Once she went inside, I checked my surroundings and went in as well. I guess she didn't notice she was being followed because she went towards the mirror doing a happy dance. I chose not to say anything yet, she looked even more attractive this close-up. As soon as I was about to walk up on her, she took her mask off catching me completely off guard.

"Samya?"

Chapter 18: You VS. Them

Samya

As soon as I heard my name, I turned around to see Jayceon staring back at me. A wave of embarrassment washed over me like a hurricane. I didn't know what to say or do. I was in shock because no one had ever seen me unmask myself at the club. I guess he was as shocked as I was.

"What the hell are you doin here?" he asked, pissed off for some apparent reason.

"I was gonna ask you the same thing."

"I'm here with friends. So, this entire time you were a stripper?"

"I don't think that's any of your damn business." I scoffed, leaning on the sink.

"So, you knew who the fuck I was when you came to Baton Rouge?"

"No, I-."

"The entire fucking time, you came down there playing the fucking victim!" he yelled making me jump.

"Jay I-."

"I don't wanna hear shit you gotta say. Here I was stressing the fuck out back home thinking our last encounter fucked things up for us but the whole time, this was some sick mind game to you. I told you about my fucking kid! I confided in you and you came there pretending like you didn't know who the fuck I was."

"It wasn't like that."

"Then tell me what the fuck it was like, huh? One thing I don't play with is people playing with my emotions."

"My intentions weren't to play with your emotions."

"Then what the fuck was it, huh? You know what fuck it, never mind. I'm not about to waste my time with you. Next time, go feed those bullshit ass stories you told to somebody else."

I had so much rage built up in me from what had been going on in my life, that I smacked him so hard, his head flew to the side. One thing I didn't like was being judged and for me to confide in him about something so traumatic and emotional that I'd been through, for him to throw it in my face, hurt to the core.

"I'm so sick and tired of people like you. People that think that they know so fucking much but got their head so stuck up they ass, that they don't know when the shut the fuck up and listen. If you would have just let me finish what the fuck, I had to say then things would have made more sense to you. I'm not even about to waste my damn breath with you." I said trying to walk past him, but he stopped me.

"I'm sorry."

"Fuck your apology, dude. Ain't your friends out there? Go before I tell your wife." I scoffed, sliding my sweats over what I had on.

"Samya, I said I'm sorry, aight?"

"And I said I don't accept. I'm tired of people apologizing

for shit that they do purposely. You meant exactly what the fuck you said, so there's no need to apologize about how you feel."

"I don't feel that way."

"Yes, you do Jayceon. Now can you get out of my way, I have to go home."

"Not until you listen to me."

"You didn't listen to me, why should I return the favor? Matter fact, why the fuck are you still here?" I replied, really getting frustrated.

I was fucking livid. You would have thought that us bumping into each other would have been cordial, but it was the opposite. I didn't know why he was mad at the shit he was mad for in general. Why was he so pissed off with me for blocking him after I'd left to go back home? What happened back at my nana house wasn't something that I wanted to happen. We were both caught in the moment and I felt bad enough that he was married, and I was doing what I was doing. One thing that I didn't want to be known as was a home wrecker or a whore. Even if he wasn't happy in his marriage, which he was, I couldn't find it in me to break up another relationship for a feeling. Just from the way he talked about his wife, I could tell there was something special.

"Because there's something about you."

"Jayceon, get out of my way before I call Eddie to throw you the fuck out of here."

"No, I'm serious, Mya. There's something about you." he replied, backing me into the wall and looking down at me.

"Like what?"

"It's something about you that keeps pulling me in. Those few months of me not talking to you or being around you made me feel alone for some reason. You may feel differently but I just can't shake it."

I stared up at him with nothing to say. He was right. I felt something when I was around him that I didn't feel around anyone else. He made me smile and feel a different type of comfort that I'd never felt before. He dealt with all my complexities and flaws that I was scared to show people. It was never easy for me to open up about the shit I'd opened up to him about. I let him in quickly because I felt a connection and it felt weird to me. I blocked him and wanted nothing else to do with him because I knew I couldn't have him. I knew there was going to be a possibility that something would go wrong, and I was scared of that. I was scared that when an ounce of happiness came my way, it would be ripped away like always; it was a pattern.

"I feel the same way, but there's nothing we can do about that."

"What if I told you that I wanted you?"

"I would tell you that you're drunk." I laughed lightly, shaking my head.

"So, if I showed you that I wanted you, how would you react?"

"Find out."

He grabbed me and picked me up, placing me on top of the sink. Stepping between my legs and grabbing my bra straps, he pulled them down exposing my breast, before sending kisses from my neck all the way down. I bit my lip trying to conceal the moan that was threatening to escape.

"Oh my God!" I moaned loudly throwing my head back, once I felt his fingers slip into my sweats, plunging into my juices.

I was praying that the music outside was loud enough so no one could hear me. I was sure that my lip was starting to draw blood from how hard I was biting it. My body wanted more but my mind was telling me that I had to stop. It was a war going on in my head and my body ended up winning in the long run. I reached for his pants and began to unbuckle them while he took his hands from my pants and tried to take his shirt off. Before we could get any further, my phone began to vibrate beside me. Looking down, I groaned, seeing Jalisa's name flash on the screen.

"I gotta go." I said quickly getting dressed.

"Why?"

"I promised my sister I would get home by a certain time. Plus, this isn't the right place to be doing this right now."

"How about I follow you home."

"I don't know about all that." I laughed lightly.

"Let me at least follow you to make sure you get there safe."

"Aren't you with your friends?'

"We bought multiple cars; they can carpool back to the hotel with somebody else."

"Okay then, let's go."

Grabbing my duffle bag and my bags full of money, I made my way out to my car and got in. Cranking it up, I pulled out of the parking lot and drove straight to my house. The entire drive, I found myself racing Jayceon and joking on the phone with him. Looking at my cell phone, I noticed Una had called me a good ten times. Thinking she was calling to talk like we'd always done around that time of night, I made a mental note to call her in the morning. Pulling into my yard, I got out and gave Jayceon the side eye when I saw him getting out of his car.

"Uh sir, you said you were going to make sure I made it home. I'm home you can go now?" I laughed.

"You're not in the house yet. Let me walk you in." he smirked, licking his lips.

"Uh no, sir, I'm fine." I laughed.

Our conversation was cut short by a car pulling into my yard so fast that it nearly knocked my mailbox over. I was getting ready to go in on who the person was that fucked up my grass with the car, until they got out. When I noticed Seven with a frantic look on his face, I grew worried.

"I thought I said I was coming to get you tomorrow."

"Look, you gotta go, we have to go. Somebody was following me!" he replied, looking around terrified.

"Seven this is a gated community. Nobody is gonna get in here without a password to the gate."

"Mya, they don't give a fuck about that! They're gonna find me!"

"Seven where's Mariah?" asked Jayceon.

"Nigga I ain't got shit to say to you. Don't worry about her." Seven replied looking at Jayceon as if he had really pissed him off.

"Seven, calm down. Listen, we're gonna go inside and then we're going to get you settled in okay?"

"You don't understan-."

His sentence was cut short by a car driving down fast and gunshots being fired. Before I could get Seven to the ground, who had his back turned, Jayceon had already tackled me to the ground and covered me.

"Get off of me! I need to go to him!" I yelled trying to get out of Jayceon's grip, but he wouldn't let me go.

Once the gunfire stopped and the car was far gone, I elbowed Jayceon in his chest and ran towards Seven, who was sprawled out on the ground with multiple gunshot wounds in him. I ran to him and pulled him into my arms rocking him. He began to wheeze and cough up blood while gripping onto me.

"No, no, no, no, no, don't you do this to me!" I cried holding him tight.

"I'm sorry."

"No Seven, come on, your gonna make it okay. You got this." I said trying to pick him up from the ground and get him to the car. Jayceon came to my side and pulled Seven's shirt up.

"He don't look good, man. Go inside and call 911, Mya." he said, looking down at the multiple wounds that were spewing blood each second.

"No! No! Get him in the car!"

"What's going on?" said Jalisa, coming outside with Rena behind her. When she saw Seven, she ran straight towards us. Her hands began to tremble as she gripped onto his bloody hand.

"What happened!" she cried, instantly looking down at him.

"Rena get her in the house."

Rena dragged Jalisa back into the house with the help of Jayceon. The last thing I needed was her putting stress on her baby. I picked Seven up with all the strength I had and pulled him into my backseat. I knew someone had already called the police, but they weren't going to make it on time. Jayceon ran back outside and I ushered him to get into the driver's seat.

"I don't know where the hospital is." he said, while peeling out of my yard.

"Use the GPS!"

"He's gonna be okay, Mya. Seven's strong."

I looked down at Seven as he was going in and out. Slapping his face, he stayed up for a split second.

"Hey, stop it. Stay awake for me, lil brother. Come on, you got this."

"I'm scared." he cried into my lap, coughing up blood.

"I know, me too. Come on man. We've been through so much; you've been through so much. You're gonna get through this."

"Please don't let me die! I don't wanna die! I can't leave my baby-." He yelled with tears in his eyes. He began to hyperventilate in my lap. I slapped his face lightly trying to get him to calm down.

"Calm down! You're not gonna die! I won't let you die."

His phone began to ring in his pocket. Reaching in and grabbing it, I noticed Una's name flashing on the screen. Answering it, I was preparing myself to tell her about what had happened moments ago.

"Seven did you get to Mya's place yet?" she sniffled

"Una! Una something bad just happened." I cried to her.

"Mya, I think Nana's dead. I came in to check on her and she won't wake up." she cried over the phone.

So much was going on in a little bit of time, that I found myself passing out in the backseat with Seven in my arms.

To Be Continued...